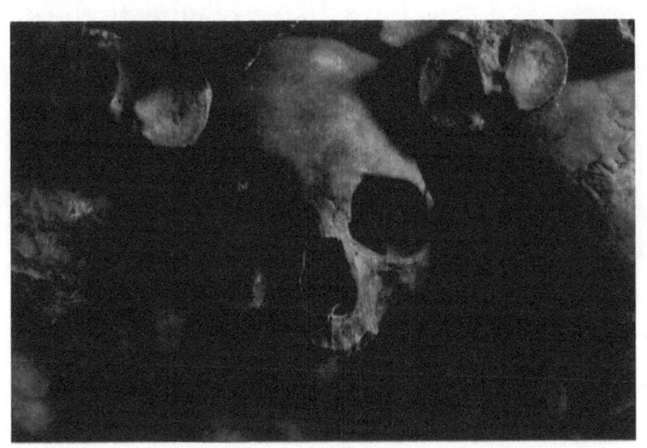

QUEEN OF BLOOD & SOULS

Raven Watters

Vampire witches aren't easy to find. They are neither enchanted, nor pure of heart.

They are creatures that hide among the magic.

But most importantly, I am an eternal beauty that will reap the souls from your sinning hearts.

Letting my darkness loose like a plague on the earth, I decide I want to see the men that have taken everything away from me pay, with their blood and souls, by being the Queen of just that.

Will the fiery flames of Hell will be the only thing to warm my cold, dead heart?

I cause quite a stir with the very mention of my presence.

Arawn not only thinks I'm his to claim, own and devour, but he also wants me to be his rogue hunter of souls, the mistress of the dark.

They underestimate a pretty face.

But never cross a wicked vampire witch, on the path of vengeance.

18+, graphic violence, sexual situations, language

Legend and Pronunciations

<u>Dearg-Due</u>: (DAH-ruhg DU-ah)
Irish mythology of a young woman who is in love with a peasant boy. Her father arranges a marriage for her to another man, she takes her own life. On the anniversary of her death, it is old that she would rise from her grave. Seeking vengeance, she visited her father and former husband while they slept. Placing her mouth over his, she sucked the life from his body and gorged herself on their blood- sustaining life. It is said that stones are placed over her grave to prevent her from rising on the anniversary of her death.
Current version: Female demon who seduces men, draining their blood.

<u>Sluagh</u>: (sloo-ah)
Irish folklore : Restless or malevolent spirits. They are the hosts of the dead, their form being similar to a flight of grey birds. They are dangerous to mortals, as they can possess them.

<u>Lord Arawn</u>: (ah-rahn)
God of Death, referred to as the 'form' in the novel. King of the Underworld, bringer of death. Makes Azalea the vampire she is. She is to leave the last drop of blood and soul. Referred to as, Soul Eater.

Raven
Watters
Romance Author

Dedicated to my friends and family that support me.
Especially to my biggest fan, Janette. I love you.

Cover art created by
John Lloyd Angcog

Raven Watters

Titles by Raven Watters

Red Haze

Destiny's Divine Plan

Crazy for his Love

Wings of Desire

Thorns of Time

Promises of Fate

Illusions of a Scarlet Scarf

Rayne: The Void Between Light and Darkness

Table of Contents

8

Prologue

The blood pools around the body of my beloved, Thomas. I continue to hold him in my arms, close to my chest. Tears roll down my face. The stench of the blood invades my nose. I raise my hand that is covering the gaping hole in the center of his chest. The blood stops flowing as he lay lifeless. The sound of his heartbeat ceases. The air no longer passing by his lips. The life blood of my love drips from my hand as I watch, silently. The rivers of red run down my arm to pool at the crook of my elbow.

The screams that have been deafening to my ears no longer ring out. The silence indicates the deaths of all around me. Why am I sitting here, breathing, not spilling my life blood on the ground?

I kiss my beloved's cheek. The smell of the rancid metallic, sticky blood on my lips. My tongue darts out to clean my bottom lip. The blood touches my tongue with a tingling sensation, tracing through my veins. I feel the vibration of my body as my heart thumps like a drum. A heat creeps into my soul, pulling, stabbing, crushing. My head falls back as I gasp for air. The need to suck in the oxygen that fades away. My heart thumps slower and slower until it stops thumping.

My head falls forward again to see the glow of the crimson blood. I kiss my beloved's cheek once more as the blackness takes over what is left of my soul. I no longer feel anything, a comfortable numbness settles in where my soul once occupied space.

"By the blood of my beloved, I vow vengeance on all that killed the only people whom I ever loved. I will drink of their blood in honor of my father." I lick the last of the blood off my lips.

A fire rages within my mind, body, and soul. I will taste the blood of all that are responsible. My eyes change as the boiling of my blood changes them from once blue to the crimson of blood, my vengeance. A surge of power fills my muscles and bones. The strength of one-hundred men flows within my veins now.

The bodies of our people lay in leave of their spirits. The souls departed from this earthly plague of man. Blood runs through the cobblestone cracks like rivers of pain and suffering.

I run my fingers along the river of blood, tasting the life of the ones I had loved. I grew hotter and hotter with each moment. The rivers of former lives fuel the anger that courses through me, for the blood of the ones responsible.

I lay my love down gently, standing there scanning the carnage left behind. My father lay nearby. The blades my father had used lay at his side. Both swords engraved of our ancestors before us. The grips made of gold, etched perfectly, adorned with rubies and diamonds. I remove the sheath from my father, strapping it to my back.

My years of training with all of the other warriors now allows me to wield the swords with expert skill. The rage within looks for some kind of release as my head falls back. My mouth wide open as the screams come from someplace deep and dark that now resides within me.

I summon for any darkness that plagues the dark skies, as the full moon is bright in the sky. The darkness overcomes every piece of my being. A hunger grows in my black smeared soul for more blood. My screams echo through the canyon of rock and trees, summoning the devil, or for death himself.

A tall dark cloaked figure appears before me, upon the back of a horse.

My blood red eyes focus on the smokey, dark figure before me. "The darkness within your soul calls to death itself. The thirst for the blood of thine enemies will stain your lips and quench your thirst in exchange for the light that remains glowing in your soul. No knife may harm you, you will have the ability of speed and agility, along with immortality. You will do the bidding that is cast upon you in times of need. Do you agree?"

My mind struggles with the blackness that now stains my soul. Everything that my mother and father had taught me of morals is naught now. Even the thoughts of my love and my parents do not elicit any feelings in me now, except more anger, hatred, and the need for revenge. "I agree."

The form reaches toward me, exposing a gray cold arm. The skin appears to be nearly translucent. You can see the black squiggly veins. "Use thine teeth to drink of my blood to seal the deal." My tongue came out to feel the two sharp teeth descending, that I will now use to rip apart the skin of my enemies, for their blood. I take the cold arm in my hands. I lower my face to the wrist of the form, stopping for a mere moment, contemplating my soul, before my teeth sink into the flesh of the form. The cold dead blood fills my mouth as he pulls his arm away.

"Only the blood of the living shall pass your lips from now on. The last drop of their blood and soul belongs to me. Daylight belongs to the living. You are now a creature of the night; you are now the Queen of the Darkness. You are the only one of your kind to do my bidding. You belong to me."

I fall to my knees as the physical pain in my body matches the mental anguish I am going through. I scream once again, shattering the silence to ward off the pain. As the pain subsides, the figure turns, vanishing from sight.

I know I must get to making me something that I can wear if I need to be in the sunlight, to completely cover my body if I can no longer be within the rays of light. The black leather will prevent the sun from touching my skin. The dark thoughts of King Carazus and his army drive my mind into madness.

My leather pants, long sleeve top and knee-high boots look like a man's outfit. I throw the cape around me, pulling the hood down over my face.

The darkness engulfing my soul grows with each thought that ravages my tortured mind and the thoughts that didn't.

The world has watched me burn, now I will watch the world burn. I will find Carazus and kill him no matter the cost. My soul gone.

Chapter 1
History of Life

Dearg Due is something that the people had called me as time went on. I walked among the people as if I belonged. They have no idea that I am always here, watching. Dearg Due is a legend in Celtic history of a young woman that loses her beloved to eventually drink the blood of her enemies. That is the condensed version. I do not have all of the time in the world, is something I cannot say now.

The king, Carazus is now my pawn in a game of cat and mouse, so to speak. As the night falls, so do his guards. Slowly one by one, I am taking everyone away, as I lure the guard to his death. My feminine ways are of immense value. My long blonde hair with stark blue eyes is too much for any of the men to resist.
Putting on a nice, but trampy dress does everything for my shapely frame. The corset top over a thin revealing shift, does the trick every time. My dress always red.

No evidence of blood and the color of the scarlet maiden. A smile and a slow walk by, looking over my shoulder does it every time. The insolent man would follow me around the corner of the castle wall.

You would think after several of the men are found around the castle walls they would stay in the walls of the castle during the nights. Men are ignorant creatures of habit. A woman learns quickly that men do not use their brain when the blood rushes to other areas of the body.

Once the ignorant arse is out of sight with me, I wrap my arms and legs around his body in a sensual lovers purpose. I sink my teeth into the flesh. The pressure of my teeth pops through the skin with the initial puncture. The more that the idiot fights, the faster his blood pumps out.

The last drop remains as he crumbles to the ground in a pile of flesh and bones. My eyes crimson like the blood I drank to sate the anger in my being.

The revenge fuels my mind to feel nothing. I pull my head away, teeth sharp with my elongated teeth. Blood smears down my chin as Arawn comes to claim his last drop and soul.

The Lord Arawn is who I come to realize, was the form that approached me as the Lord of Death, the soul eater, my creator, my captor, my master now. His large framed looking gray body covered in a black robe, leans over the body of my victim. He places his hand over the chest of the victim to summon the soul for his own.

The soul, a bright white light of the man that was, raises out of his now empty body to become a ball of light, held in the hand of Arawn. One drop of blood is smudged on the bright white ball that is his soul. Lord Arawn holds up the ball of light in his hand to then open his mouth, which stretches to disgusting proportion to place the ball into his mouth. He swallows as the light of the soul disappears into the oblivion of the soul eater.

Talk among the people indicates that a woman is seen to lure these men into the shadows to then drink his blood and eat his soul. Legend says the Dearg Due is a soul eater. Others say they have seen the tall, dark, robed figure, be the soul eater. The legends became increasingly exaggerated.

The time for my revenge approaches as Arawn tells me the next soul to go would be the son of King Carazus. Slightly disappointed it is not the king himself; this kill will be just as sweet. To watch the kings reaction, to his only son and heir to the throne; die by my hand. The king should remember the face of the one that takes his beloved son, just as I see the face of the one who killed my beloved Thomas every day, in every dream, in everything I do.

A celebration is planned for the prince to celebrate his twenty-first birthday and his right to the kingdom, as his father Carazus will step down. I cannot have his son take the throne. He is probably more evil than his father. He has taught him well.

As a gift from the king, Prince Vincent will have five women of his choice to be sent to his chambers for his pleasure. The cruelty went as far as to any woman, married or not, would have to comply. The extent of their cruelty knows no limits.

Dressed in my best. I make sure to go to the castle early to get in front of the crowd. He will notice me. No matter if I have to mesmerize him with my powers bestowed upon me. I know that Prince Vincent is very handsome, due to his mother of course. His dark hair long with curl in it. Blue eyes match the sky. Strong features. She will be able to enjoy this one before she drinks all of his blood.

The hustle and bustle of the castle keeps everyone busy as I plan what I will need to do. My gown of a deep green from my ancestors colors. My bodice makes my breasts pop up and out more. The notice I will have with this dress is exactly what I want. The looks of the socialites let me know that my choice of dress, long blonde hair in curls, with red lips, are the right ones.

I was able to sneak into the room of the prince to get a layout of it. The extravagant furniture of intricately carved wood and gold inlay. The enormous four poster bed sat against the wall with the ability for privacy. On the other side of the room was a walk-in tub area, large enough for at least ten people.

The water now clean and filled with rose petals for the prince to have the pleasures that he so chooses to take. I see the bottles of wine to be drank by all. I suppose some of the women would be drinking more wine than they should, due to the situation.

I uncork the wine bottles to add the sleeping potion I have made. My eyes change to a crimson as I cast my spell for the potion. "I cast thee to drift off to sleep with a sip. Prince Vincent shall remain awake. Blessed be, as above, shall be below."

The scene now ready and set for whatever happens. I am willing to give my life to rid the world of theirs. The evil of the king and his son needs to have an end in sight. The torture of the people and the lands needs to stop.

I realize at this moment that I held more than grudge. I also hold a purpose in my life. No matter what is left of it. My purpose is of ridding the world of the tyrants, once and for all.

Chapter 2
History of Living

The people of the castle buzz, but not in a good way. Prince Vincent had run his sword through a castle worker that made him angry. His dark soul had no limits as to the misery he spread without prejudice. The worker had been a middle-aged woman that had two children. No matter how dark my soul had become, I still knew the feeling of misery, pain, and anguish. I suffer from it on a daily basis.

Arawn aches to possess the soul of Vincent. The blackness he carries will sate his hunger many times over. The darker the soul, the better it makes him feel. He explained to me that his power comes from the light of the souls he eats, but the darker the better, for a rush almost orgasmic. The power of the darkness feeds his hunger not power. The light I have left in my soul is what he seeks within me. The light to keep his powers strong. Each innocent soul he devours gives him the power of immortality.

The guests of the castle all sit at the enormous tables lavished with food of all kinds, while the wards of the kingdom are starving. The enormous table has a complete roasted hog with an apple in its mouth in the center. Fruits of all kinds litter the table with goblets of wine and mead for the celebration.

The meal will end with the appointment of the new king of Theesland. King Carazus sits at the head of one end of the table with Vincent at the other end. Both men laughing their guttural laughs with food leaving their mouth in the form of spittle. With every bite came a laugh and more food out of their vile mouths.

Both the king and the prince sport a long beard that is now catching all of the food that they have not chewed or lost out of their mouth while talking. The bile rises up in my throat as I watch the drips of red wine travel down their beards to fall upon their robes of velvet and the finest threads.

The meal ends abruptly as King Carazus stands, bellowing at the top of his lungs, "It is time to let Vincent have his commencements. Everyone gets to go to the chapel for the official part." The crowd exits the great hall to fill the chapel for the coronation of the new king.

I stand back with all of the others that have been invited. I had to mimic another invitation that had been sent out to another that I had paid a visit to.

Arawn was anxious for me to provide Lady Helena's blood and soul to him. Her blood stained with the alcohol that poisoned her liver. I had to choke down the putrid blood as she lay there in a state of dying. Arawn took pleasure in the removal of her dark soul.

The guests all kneel as King Carazus and Prince Vincent walk past, to approach the altar in the chapel. I happen to look up as they are passing. With that small glance, Vincent notices me. He stops for a moment as I bat my eyes at him. The bile I am choking down from disgust is nearly intolerable as I act like I like him to make sure I have caught his attention for later.

I exaggerate a side smile like an innocent would, shyly. He smiles a wicked smile before continuing to follow his father to the altar. My stomach churns upon itself as I know what I must do. Thank the gods he has a handsome face. His eyes as black as the obsidian of his heart and soul as he shows his lust.

Carazus removes his crown, as a crown is placed upon the head of Vincent. Carazus will retain his crown as a new one is made for the new king. The kings wizard is placed in charge of maintaining that magic is not bestowed upon the crown during the process in which it is made.

The ceremony concludes with Vincent kneeling and kissing the ring of the king he is succeeding. The ring then placed on his finger. The left ring finger, where married women are forced to wear a ring to represent, they are married.

The lust for his blood is driving me to the brink of madness. The insatiable need to sink my teeth into his tender flesh as I take the life out of his body. I will make sure to make the process last as long as possible. He will be in ecstasy as he becomes weaker and weaker, until I watch his eyes dim increasingly until his final drop remains as well as his black heart and soul.

The former king, Carazus yells to the crowd. "All of the women who are present are to come to the front of the pews and kneel before your new king. He will choose the women to meet his needs.

I kneel at the end of the pew as all the other women have done. I wait and watch as he walks up to each woman, grabbing her chin to direct her face upwards, to gaze upon it. He stops at a young girl of maybe fifteen, motioning for her to move to the back of the room. The scoundrel of a man wants the innocence of the younger girls. I on the other hand know that no matter what, he must choose me as well.

King Vincent approaches me with quicker steps as he notices me. He grabs my chin between his thumb and forefinger to lift my face upward to him. His blue eyes once again turn dark with lust. He looks into my eyes, waiting for something. I slightly lift the corner of my mouth, enticing him with the tip of my tongue darting out to wet my lips. That was all it took for him to let go of my face, grabbing my upper arm, dragging me with him to the back of the room where he motions for the others to follow along.

The young girls follow us as he keeps hold of my arm. The door to his room opens up as we approach. Most of the younger girls are shoved into the room as they resist. Several servants hold the door and many sit along the edge of the inset tub. Others wait with bottles of wine and glasses. They begin to poor glasses of wine as the girls take a glass each.

Vincent proposes a toast to his rule as the new

king and the night ahead, with a disgusting sneer upon his lips.

We toast as I hold the glass to my lips without drinking. Most of the younger girls drink the entire glass as quickly as possible. I take things into my own hands as the hunger for blood starts to take over my thinking. With the young innocent girls around, my stomach growled for fresh innocent blood. I have my eyes on another target though.

I start to undress as Vincent watches. His eyes darken with lust as he matches my movements of taking clothing off. In a few moments we are both undressed as the servant had helped me to unlace my corset in a timely manner. I walk my naked body toward the steaming water. The servants that sit beside the tub hand me another glass of wine.

I reject the wine as the strong arm of Vincent comes around my waist, holding tightly. I look over his shoulder as I see many of the girls are staggering around the room with the servants attempting to assist them. I cast another spell, "all that occupy this room are to follow suit of the wine."

Vincent roars in my ear, asking what I said. "Nothing my king. I was simply purring in your ear. I was hoping you would choose me to return to your chambers with you." I purr the words into his ear as I breathe in deeply of the scent of his blood.

29

King Vincent has the body of a king, such a waist of great human flesh on such a vulgar man. His erection stands perfectly at attention as I lower myself onto him. He lays back against the side as I move just enough to cause him to moan. He attempts to lean up to grab me as I push him back, slapping his hands away. He growls with acceptance as I ride him until the tightening in the pit of my core is ready to unravel.

Vincent reaches up, grabbing a handful of my hair with one hand as he wraps an arm around my waist. His mouth descends onto my neck as the unraveling starts. The servants and other women are all passed out around the room. My eyes turn crimson as my teeth start their descent. My teeth sharp and my actions quick.

My core starts to unravel at my climax as I sink my elongated teeth into the neck of Vincent. His immediate reaction is to wrap both arms around me and squeeze. I bite harder as he continues to lose more blood with his heart rate increasing. My orgasm reaches a new height with the combination.

Vincent stops fighting so much as he is weakened from the loss of the blood, I have taken in from him. I pull my head back to feel the pulse of his body inside of me as he orgasmed as well. "Such a waste. We could do this more often. I cannot let you go yet though. I need to make you suffer as I ride out what you have left within you. You remain hard from the rapid loss of blood, except from the area holding blood. Too bad your heart and brain are not the same way." I move on him again as the water sloshes around us. His eyes roll back in ecstasy as he attempts to talk. No words come out, only a moan.

I continue to build to my orgasm again as I plunge my teeth into the other side of his neck. I drink slowly as I feel my release again. I move my body, so I look into the cloudy eyes of King Vincent. "You will never hurt another again. May you not rest in peace. The soul eater has come for you. Your black, hideous soul is no longer your own." I feel his heartbeat slow more as Arawn appears before me.

"It appears you have completed another task for me successfully. Such a good girl you are. Glad you were able to enjoy yourself." I use my strength to pick Vincent up, out of the water, tossing him onto the floor in front of Arawn. I nonchalantly walk out of the tub to obtain my clothing I hid in the room earlier.
Arawn watches me walk away as he chuckles. The sound raises the hairs on the back of my neck and arms. I turn to see what he is doing. He is watching me.

"Like what you see?" I put my top on.

"You are an amazing specimen for your duties to the true soul eater. You lure a man to his death with your beauty in the eyes of man. You are magnificent. If

I were of humankind, I would claim your body for my own. You have not failed me yet." The dark smoke and shadows in the room disappear with his departure. I wipe the blood from my chin with my hand, washing it in the tub.

I exit out of the window as I had planned earlier with my scouting trip. The guards will all be in the main hall eating and drinking until their glutenous bodies have had enough.

Chapter 3
History of Death

I am on the edge of the kingdom as I hear the screams of whomever found the scene in the new king's chambers. I am sure that there is some cheering involved with those screams. Next Carazus. At least for now my thirst sated with a much-needed long nap. I return to my dwelling as you could call it.

The dwelling I occupy is located at the base of the mountains. A humble small cottage within the thick tree cover. The trees so thick that the sun cannot permeate the area. The foliage of ferns so thick you have to wade through them to reach the cottage.

The heavy door creaks as it opens. I leave it that way in case someone happens upon me. The lantern lights the room that contains only a small table with a couple of chairs. The fireplace small but unused. A large rug covers the wood floor. Most homes have dirt floors. I specifically made a wood floor to cover the hatch that the rug covers for me to rest in. My chamber had been dug out to about the entire size of the cottage, with an escape path out into the dense forest. I no longer respond to the cold as I had before. The cold no longer affected me.

Herbs hang around the ceiling to dry. I may need to drink blood to survive, but I did practice witchcraft prior to the death of my beloved Thomas.
I continue to wonder to this day, why I, of all people did survive. I was the sole survivor of that attack. Was it a divine intervention, luck, or something else? I am sure I will never have the answers I seek. I choose to believe that The Soul Eater, God Arawn chose me to do his bidding. Leaving me to live in torment. To have mercy, would have been to die that day with everyone else I loved.

My former life remained unknown to myself. I suppose I may have been the villain then. My punishment for the sins of my past or that of my parents. I lost my mother at an incredibly early age. I grew up with my father and my aunt to raise me. Mother came down with a sickness that took her from us.

I enter my chamber below the cottage access door covered with the rug. I had structured a small sleeping area on a bed of sorts I had made out of wood with an earthy covering. I found more comfort than lying on the cold, hard earth.

I lay on my bedding of moss and pine branches, covered with furs to snuggle into the comfort. My mind drifts to my past. I do not remember how long ago my 'past' is. I know that King Carazus did not have a child yet. That had been nearly 22 years ago. The time has passed with the blink of an eye. Immortality is loneliness. The only good part is the not aging and your body heals itself quickly. Otherwise, she would have rather gone to the great beyond with her family and the man she loved.

The darkness surrounds me in a blanket of happiness.

Picking the vegetables out of the garden causes my lower back to hurt with all of the bending. I stand upright to place my hand to my lower back, stretching the pain out. The sun is warm on my face, as I wipe the beads of sweat from my brow. The challenging work is all worth it in the end. I smile at the thought of fresh vegetables.

Father is working the ground outside of the garden for the wheat that we need for an income. We buy our essentials with that money. My father Tobias is a hard-working man that is showing his age from years of that arduous work and exposure to the rays of the sun. His hands rough with calluses as long as I can remember.

Thomas Victor has been a part of our lives for many years now. Thomas had lost his family to a sickness that he never did get. Father took him in as a teenager to help out with the land. Thomas and I grew closer and closer as I became a young woman of eighteen, he asked if I would marry him. Father was over the moon with the approval of our union.

The wedding is to take place in one month's time with the rising of the full moon. The plans are going well for things to go as scheduled. The landowners all help each other out. The other landowners are all to be present with the gift of food. The duke of our lands has donated a hog. He and the Duchess are truly kind and generous to all of the landowners surrounding them.

Arrangements for the celebration are all falling into place now. The time is quickly approaching.

Thomas and I would sneak off at nights to have some time alone. We would go to the water's edge to have our alone time. It was within those visits that we would make love.

Our first time was so romantic. I was so shy about everything, but the thought of his touch now sends waves of excitement through my body like a lightning bolt hitting me. I cannot wait until we can build our own cottage near to father so we can have our own family.

The night skies light up like the sun rising. The sun should not rise for at least another hour. We all get out of our beds as Father looks out in the direction of the light. The light is emanating from the castle of the duke and duchess. Others exit their cottages as well with the light and the loud sounds of screams.

We arrive at the castle just as the sun starts to rise. Every landowner from the area fights with sword and shield beside all of the castle knights. We know most of the knights due to being there for the markets. The knights train daily just outside of the castle walls. The landowners usually train with them. I was not supposed to be there, but I wanted to learn to fight too, if necessary.

The sun rises over the sounds of the screams with the enemy directly in front of the rising sun. The shadows of the enemy casting over the castle walls for eerie figures of men with horned helmets.

I pick up a sword at my feet, from a knight that was run through by the enemies sword. His eyes cloudy and lifeless

37

with blood pooling out of his mouth. A rage flares up from somewhere deep within me. I have never felt anything like it.

I feel like I have superhuman power. The blade seems to vibrate with my touch.

I know the magic that resides within me will take over. The power running in my veins will summon something much worse than that of the king and his men. I fight with the fear of the power taking over my entire being.

I swing the blade true as a man approaches me. His chest opens, as the muscle and fat tissue open, with the flow of blood. He falls to the ground with a thump, gripping his chest to take his final breath. The exhilaration of the adrenaline rush fogs my brain. I am unable to think clearly.

I continue to swing my blade, killing all that come before me. The enemy keeps coming as if there is no end to them. I glance around to see that most of our landowners and knights are now dead or dying in the very soil they love and fight to keep.

A terrible pain fills my head of earth-shattering proportions. I feel as if my skull just split open. Blood runs down my face, over my eyes and mouth to drip to the ground. For some reason I look down as the ground quickly approaches my face. The pain is all that I can think about, I hear the screams, smell the metallic of the blood all around me as the darkness takes me.

I open my eyes once again to see the carnage of the battle. The blood pools around the body of my beloved, Thomas. I gather him in my arms, holding him close to my chest. Tears roll down my face. The stench of the blood invades my nose. I raise my hand that is covering the gaping hole in the center of his chest. The blood stops flowing as he lay lifeless. The sound of his heartbeat ceases. The air no longer passing by his lips. The life blood of my love drips from my hand as I watch. The rivers of red run down my arm to pool at the crook of my elbow.

The screams that have been deafening to my ears no longer ring out. The silence indicates the deaths of all around me. Why am I sitting here, breathing, not spilling my life blood on the ground? How long have I been laying here? I kiss my beloved's cheek. The smell of the rancid metallic, sticky blood on my lips. My tongue darts out to clean my bottom lip. The blood touches my tongue with a tingling sensation, tracing through my veins. I feel the vibration of my body as my heart thumps like a drum. A heat creeps into my soul, pulling, stabbing, crushing. My head falls back as I gasp for air. My scream echoes through the castle halls among the dead to muffle the sound. The need to suck in the oxygen that fades away. My heart thumps slower and slower until it stops thumping.

The dream and memories of the past will haunt me forever and a day. I may have lost my soul, but I have not lost myself, not yet. I feel the darkness start to consume me at times. The darkness of what my soul used to be and will be forever more now. Once the darkness consumes the mind, the body will follow.

The reminders of why and who I am wash over me with a lifetimes worth of regrets and anguish. The emptiness that surrounds the darkness is all consuming if you stare into the abyss long enough.

Chapter 4

Azalea: My Personal Prison

I sit straight up in the bed, breathing heavily. Nightmares come every time I close my eyes to rest. Hence the lack of rest. I live through the anguish over and over again. The only reason I still remain is due to the need for revenge that I have still not been able to obtain. Arawn has kept me at bay. He thinks that if I achieve my revenge that I will no longer bring him souls.

I hear the most minuscule amount of sound, due to my enhanced hearing, from my creaky front door into the cottage. I wait, listening for more sound. I track the sound above me with my eyes, the tapping of light footsteps. I pad quietly to the escape route to the outside.

I reach the opening of the escape route to have something thrown over my head. A burlap sack of sorts with the sound of a whip snapping in the air, tangling itself around my ankles. My arms grabbed and are being held to each side of me.

I let out a shrill scream that mortal ears cannot tolerate. My arms are released, I pull the burlap sack off of my head. I see the king's flag colors, knowing that the game has now begun. I unwrap the whip off of my ankles while the men are all still rolling on the ground, holding their hands over their ears.

I take hold of the nearest sword. My eyes turn crimson with the anger that boils inside of me now. My teeth protrude as I attack the closest man. I ran the sword through his gut as I leaned over plunging my teeth into the side of his neck. I will need all of the strength I can get right now. The man lay lifeless as I throw my head back, the blood surges through my body.

The renewal from the fresh innocent blood empowers my renewed strength and speed. The effects of the scream are starting to wear off as some of the men get to their knees to get up. I grab the next with my hand around his neck. I lift him up so that my teeth sink into his lower neck.

The blood trickles down the front of his armor. I close my eyes for a moment to get my sword, which lays in wait to bring forth the blood of the enemy. My sword will appear with the magic and spell. "Thine sword of vengeance of my ancestors, bestow yourself upon me now." I hold out my right arm as the sword appears.

Several men are watching as this happens, they run for safety. I feel the sting of a sword blade running through my mid-section from behind me. The tip of the sword protrudes from my stomach in the front. I step forward a few steps as the blade pulls out of my body. I had to pull hard with the suction of my flesh around the blade.

I turn to the young man standing there with his mouth gaping, sword still being held in place, and wide eyes. His expression of sheer fear.

"Are you a coward young sir? You dare to attack me from behind. You have learned better than that in battle practice I hope." I am behind him in a flash with my mouth next to his ear. I whispered into his ear. "Do you have any idea who I am?" I am waiting for an answer. "Can you talk?" He only nods his head as the tip of one of my teeth scrapes along his neck.

Several men stand there watching to see what I am going to do next. A thin line of blood appears from the scratch. I stick the tip of my tongue out to trace the line of blood. I hear the young man take a deep breath in as I feel his body quiver beneath me. I do not know whether he quivers in desire or in fear. I hope for both. My body vibrates with desire and anticipation .

I no longer feel fear, more of, the anticipation of what the moment will bring. The shiver of the young man's desire brought my body to the orgasmic state that only his flesh and blood would satisfy.

I lean into his neck as I run my hand up the front of his neck. His head falls back with no fight. "You are not worthy of me letting you live. You are a coward. You hinder the king's knights." I run my sharp thumb nail down the side of his windpipe to gouge into the artery. The blood oozes out forcefully with each heartbeat. I take in the blood that now leaves his body without a sound.

The men watching have swords, ropes, and chains in an attempt to obviously capture me. "What are you boys planning on doing with those? Are we going to do naughty things?" I approach the men slowly as I cast a spell of compliance over them. My crimson eyes and immortal power will mesmerize any mortal. I drag my sword behind me as the tip digs into the ground, carrying pine needles along. My hips sway to the beat of thine own drum in my head.

The display of men in front of me, stand there awaiting their demise. A man steps out from behind them with a robe on, arm raised in front of himself. Several sluagh appear from above. The sunlight peeks through the treetops in flashes with the sluaghs' descent. The smell of rot penetrates the area.

The man in the robe with his hood guarding his face looks up pulling his hood down. I recognize the wizard Elzabus. He had been much younger and part of the good practices at one time. He has always been immensely powerful. I cannot compete with his magic.

"Why are you here with the men of Carazus, Elzabus?" I let my fangs retreat as my eyes return to blue. My long blonde hair hanging in a braid to the side.

"Hello Azalea. You have been a very naughty girl. The king wishes to have you returned to the castle for your punishment."

"You mean my death, you coward? You have aged since I last saw you, old man. Why would you help the enemy that destroyed our home and lives?" I sneer at him for his treachery.

"Not much else an old wizard can do after they lose everything. Have you seen what you have become Azalea? You are a monster now. You were always such a loving, beautiful girl. Thomas would be disappointed right now."

I move faster than any eye could see, as I step behind Elzabus with a blade to his throat. I stand behind him seething in anger. "You do not have the right to speak about Thomas or my father, anybody for that matter. Where were you that morning of the attack by King Carazus?" I push the length of the blade harder against his throat. The motion of him swallowing moves the knife up and down with its movement.

The sluagh circle above our heads. The souls of the tormented. Some may have been from my doing. I am sure they are. Elzabus knew the only way to contain me is to use the sluagh. The descent of a flock of birds gathers into a form to circle above us.

"You know you cannot stay in this state Azalea. You have done your bidding enough for Arawn. You have not been able to exact your revenge as was agreed upon. Retract your agreement and pass on to the next realm of life. You deserve happiness. I know you miss Thomas with all of what you have."

A tear runs down my face. I did not think I could still cry or feel anything other than anger and disgust now. It has been so long since I have had any other emotions or even thought about Thomas or my father.

"I have a plan for you Azalea. I owe you that much. You have become this monster because of my doing. I cannot cure you of your affliction, but I can hide you for the king to never find you. Arawn will not be able to find you either. You will have the time you need to heal mentally from this trauma."

I ease the blade away from his throat a bit more as he speaks to me. I had looked up to this man for so long when I was younger. I wanted to be just like him when I was a young child, so respected and powerful. My hand holding the blade against his throat continues to move away slowly.

"Do you trust me, Azalea? I promise I will not let any harm befall to you."

I motion my arm across the men stating, "sleep." Every man drops to the ground asleep with my power.

"I see you have become stronger in your powers. I am proud of you for that. You could have been a great apprentice. I need you to get ready to go now."

I return in a few moments with my leather on, and my black hooded robe. I pull the hood over my head like Elzabus, as we head up the mountainside.

Rocks fall around us with our climb. The sluagh continues to gain more souls as it circles close to us. Several times I catch Elzabus as his foot slips on the loose rocks.

The climb ends with us stepping up onto a ledge with a cave on the side of the mountain, as Elzabus speaks a spell. An opening in the mountainside opens large enough to walk through. He lights a torch as we enter the darkness.

We walk for several feet into the side of the mountain as he turns looking toward me. He hands me the torch as he reaches into the satchel that he carries with him. "I have a potion here for you to take. You have to trust me. Please hear me out. This potion will suppress your powers and magic so that it is undetectable. It will make you asleep for a long time.

Arawn will have moved on to his next servant of darkness. Carazus will not live much longer, he has been poisoned by yours truly." He fumbles in his satchel until he turns the direction of the wood frame of a bed like the one, I rest in.

"I will also cast a spell on you with the potion. Are you willing to do this? I would rather not see you burned or beheaded Azalea." He glances down with remorse on his face.

I detect the sound of men talking, coming up the side of the mountain. I handed the torch over to Elzabus to go check. He does not hear the men like I can. Looking over the edge, rocks fall and tumble down the mountainside. The army of Carazus is ascending the mountain quickly.

"The men of Carazus' are almost here." I return to Elzabus' side.

"Quickly, drink this now and lay down there. I will cast the spell, then seal the cave. No one will know we have been here. Do not worry about me."

I look to Elzabus, not quite trusting him, but I know I do not have much choice. I lift the vial of bitter smelling liquid to swallow the even more bitter taste of the potion. It took everything I had to not heave the insides of my stomach, which consists of the blood of several men.

I lay on the makeshift bed; I feel different somehow. My body feels more numb than it had before. How can that be? The words seem to spill out of his mouth as I watch him, unable to move now. He holds his staff above my body, making an infinity symbol. "Let this creature heal herself mentally from her tortures. Let her sleep the sleep of the dead to raise with the return of her love once again."

Instantly, I realize what he had just said. My love was not coming back. I went into a panic too late as I saw him step out onto the rock ledge to leap off. The opening of the cave closing behind him, filling in with rock and dirt. There is no way anyone will ever find me. Elzabus is the only one that knows where I am, and now he is gone.

There is a feeling of impending doom as the walls close in around me. I close my eyes against the

dirt coming in around the cocoon of rocks protecting
my body.

Chapter 5

Sterling

The entire room full of students watch as I, the honored guest, Professor Sterling Mason, unwraps the cloth from my latest find. The piece will be taken to the museum after we are done examining it. The book of; The King Carazus by his wizard, Elzabus.

I have waited for this moment for all of my adult life. The research had shown that King Carazus ruled with an iron fist for too many years. Legends of a book of spells and the life of the king, from his trusted wizard. The stories tell that his wizard mysteriously disappeared into the Keldane Mountains of Ireland to never be seen again.

This book may be the key to the wizard Elzabus' disappearance and why he left the king. A few legends talk about King Carazus being a tyrant that would have bathed in blood if he had the chance. Stories to the other end of the spectrum spoke of the great king he was.

Running my hands through my dark hair, curls spring back into my face, going over one of my golden colored eyes, as I apply my white felt gloves to touch the book.

So many questions and here lies the answers; I hope. I will never admit how I obtained this book and received it. --Someone digging around an area they do not want shut down for artifacts having been found. If the authorities find out, the digging would be stopped.-- I have the money though. I don't even have to work after the death of my grandfather.

Thoughts of my grandfather, that I was named after, causes a tightening in my chest. My grandfather was the biggest part of my life. I loved my grandfather dearly. He would tell stories to me all the time, of the wizard and king. Grandfather used to carry on that we are direct descendants of the Wizard Elzabus. Hence the reason I now stand in Ireland's University with my treasure.

Grandfather Sterling spent most of his adult life as an archeologist as well, with his specialty in Celtic history. I decided to walk in my grandfather's shoes when I grew up. Grandfather made sure that I had only the finest and best education in the world. I have traveled abroad for most of my studies of course.

My penthouse in New York City sits empty most of the time. My housekeeper will go over and keep an eye on the place for me when I am out of town. Being a guest speaker at the University is quite a privilege. Hoping for the students to dive in with as much passion and excitement as I have. I can use some help at a dig in the Keldane Mountains. I need others with the hunger that I have for the history.

I take a deep breath as the students are gathered around the table watching with anticipation. The leather-bound book is in pristine condition. It looks as if it has been kept in an airtight place. The white gloves turn the keeper on the book for it to open. The old spine of the book crackles and echoes in the silence of the room.

I let out my breath as the book opens up to the statement that this journal belongs to the wizard Elzabus with connotations of the life of the king Carazus. The paper made crinkling sounds with the turn of each one.

Most of the pages had spells that the wizard would perform for varied reasons. Anxious to read more about the wizard's personal life, I scan the pages with interest. The story goes on to talk about him living among the landowners and others that have magic within them.

A story emphasizes a premonition that the kings army would be attacking a castle of the local Duke and Duchess, purpose unknown. The wizard left the landowners alone for that period of time. When he returned to his home with his wife that carried his child, he found all of them dead, slaughtered uselessly by the king, except one woman Azalea.

Azalea is described to be the next most powerful witch to Elzabus, but she is unaware of her abilities. "She sought vengeance and revenge on king Carazus for the death of her loved ones and her beloved Thomas. She makes a deal with Death, Arawn in return for revenge on the king. She would provide souls for Death also known as the 'soul eater.' She was to have life sustaining power and immortality from the blood of the mortals. Hence forth like the Dearg Due. She is known to be, The Queen of Blood and Souls." I shift uncomfortably onto my other foot.

An image of a beautiful blonde woman with bright blue eyes flashes into my mind. A woman of such beauty that she takes my breath away, just gazing upon her. Another flash in my mind of blood running down her chin with crimson eyes, fangs, and a black hooded cape.

The vision of the woman makes my heartbeat faster and heavier than it has before. I have never had time for a relationship. I am always on the road and busy. My mother is the only family I have left now. The complaints of my mother to settle down and have children falls upon deaf ears.

The pages continue with more spells. Something catches my attention. Out of the corner of my eye, from outside the window, a flock of grey birds move in a strange pattern, as if in waves and shapes. They plummet toward the ground to ascend just as quickly up again. A scream echoes in my head with the vision of the flock of birds. The scream is painful to my ears. I cover my ears with my hands in an attempt to silence it. The screams fade away as the flock of birds fly out of my sight.

Returning my attention back to the book, I look up to the feeling that I am being watched. The entire classroom of people are looking at me in confusion. I shake my head and continue talking about what I am reading in the book. The final spells in the book talk of the wizard having the ability to speak to this book, to document what he says. The final passage in the book is of him talking to Azalea within a mountain.

"That does not make much sense that he is talking to her within a mountain. There is mention of a small cottage at the bottom of the mountain. His death came quickly as he stepped off of the ledge of the mountain." Well, any clue is better than none, I thought to myself.

I decided that I need to find out more as to where this was found. There has to be something else left of him, his skeletal remains maybe. Some evidence of what happened to him. I need to know more about this Azalea. I need to look through my grandfather's library.

I slept most of the flight back home. After a layover in France. I had just enough time to do a little shopping I needed and get an amazing coffee or two in me before my flight left. I lazily walked along the water's edge, thinking about the blond-haired, blue-eyed woman in my visions.

I had not told my mother that I had been having some strange dreams and visions lately. I would sometimes wake up in the middle of the night, not sure where I was. I had imagined a book that appeared to me. I thought for sure that my mind had made that one up. There is no way that people can summon objects from thin air, making them materialize. Mother never believed in anything super-natural.

My limo driver, Dirk, was waiting at the airport for me as I stepped out of the terminal. I pack light, not much to carry and nothing to claim.

"We are headed to the estate before we go back to the penthouse, Dirk." I climb into the back of the limo, taking my phone out to call the housekeeper to let them know I am headed there.

The drive to the estate is breathtaking with the trees and foliage. Pulling up to the gates of the estate, memories flood back to me about my time here with my grandfather. The adventures, stories, and time together. I never had a father around. My father left my mother and I not long after I was born. My male figure was then of course my grandfather. He always apologized to me that my father had done that to us. Facts be known, he deserted his father as well.

The iron gates open slowly as Tim the groundskeeper slides them to the side. The estate is hundreds of years old, grandfather liked to maintain the nostalgia of the past. The driveway to the house remains the cobblestone, hand laid years ago. It is maintained without fail. All the stones of grays to reds. A thing of beauty is what my grandfather would say every time we came through the gates.

The front entrance into the house has a couple of pillars with a wide, rounded edge staircase to the French doors. Every room has a small patio with wrought iron railings. Floor to ceiling windows in the main living areas. The estate has always been my sanctuary. I always wondered if the estate was haunted. As a child I would hear or see things while in the hallways. Always a black hooded figure.

Betsy opens the door for me to enter, just as if I were still a small child. She has been like family to me my entire life. There was never a time that she was not there when I was. When grandfather passed away, she requested and asked to stay living and working on the estate. There was no way that I would allow her to go anywhere else.

Chapter 6

Sterling: Investigating the Past

Entering the library was a bit like stepping back in time. The smells of the paper in the books, the leather-bound books, the wood of the shelves. Visions of watching my grandfather sitting at the large desk, reading something, researching another myth. Preparing for another trip to dig something else up. It hurts to think of my grandfather being gone now. The library is simply different now than it was before.

I enter, shutting the library doors for some privacy, approaching the desk to look through whatever grandfather had been looking at when he had died of the heart attack. He had always been as healthy as a horse before then. It was definitely a shock for him to be found right here on this very library floor, dead from a heart attack.

This is the first time since the funeral, almost a year ago, that I have been able to step into the library. Without a doubt, the library is my grandfather.

Scattered around the desk were papers that had illustrations of the book that I now possess. My grandfather knew what it looked like. "You knew all along what it looked like old man?" I often speak aloud as if my grandfather is listening and going to respond. "As a matter of fact. I just found out what the book looked like. I can't believe you would call me old man!" A quirk in his voice at the last comment.

I stand in my spot not moving for a few moments, eyes closed, wondering why I imagine my grandfather is talking to me. "Maybe it was not the right time to come into the library or the estate yet. If my mind is going to play tricks on me, then I should probably go to the penthouse now. I hope I have not gone crazy."

"You are not crazy or delusional my boy. I am talking to you. I have been waiting for you to come back. I am happy to see you. You look well."

Running my hands through my thick dark hair as I take a deep breath, several times. "I think I have lost my shit." I turned around slowly to look in the direction of the voice that sounded like my grandfather.

I stumble back several steps to fall back onto the desk, falling back onto it as I gaze upon my grandfather's apparition. He looks like grandfather, just kind of like 'see through.' I shake my head several times to clear any misgivings of my sight. A confused look comes over my face. I look around the library, seeing all of the books on their shelves, in place. My eyes dart back to the spot that my grandfather occupied, to discover him still standing there.

Standing back up, straight, and tall, I shake my head and blink several times again. Still there? "Ok, so I have lost my mind or now I am conversing with my deceased grandfather. The blonde of my visions has created hallucinations for my mind."

"So, you have seen her? I have been hoping to have her come to me in visions. She is obviously drawn to you. She is in a perpetual state of dream walking right now." The apparition of my grandfather paces before my very eyes. "The only option is for us to find her. Are you ready for an adventure, my boy?"

"All of the information I have obtained from the wizard Elzabus and Azalea is on my desk. I believe that I have found the final resting place of both of them." The pacing continues as he rambles on about the two of them.

I took a chance to reply to my grandfather. "So, if you figured it out, why didn't you go there?"

"I did not get the chance; the ticker took a turn for the worse. I did not take care of myself like I should have. I was always on the go, looking and searching for our ancestors."

"So, you know for sure they are our ancestors?" I look to my grandfather with skepticism. "I really need a stiff drink right now."

"I know that they are. I traced our ancestors back until them. It was at least 1,500 years ago. There may not be anything left of their bones, but maybe some evidence in the area."

I am looking at my grandfather questioningly. "I just have so many questions. This really shouldn't be happening. Impossible actually. I still think I may have lost my mind along the way."

"What would you like to know? What happens when you die? Where I should have gone?"

"Slow down grandpa." I walk around the large desk to sit in the oversized chair. The leather creaked with it moving from my weight. I jumped back up immediately. "This is your chair grandpa."

"It is yours now my boy. I cannot really sit anyway." He starts chuckling at his own joke. He did not lose his sense of humor with death.

"Okay, so, how exactly is this possible?" I sat back in the chair again. "How can you be here like you are right now? Why have I never seen a 'spirit' before?

Are you a spirit or something else? I have so many questions and thoughts." I hang my head as I shake it. I thought maybe I just needed to clear my head.

"I have been asking myself the same question. I keep coming back to the fact that I have unfinished business. I know that is so cliché. I have no other explanations than, it is meant to be for me to stay with you for now. There has to be some higher purpose."

My grandfather stops pacing for a few seconds. "Have you been having any weird dreams or like, visions lately? Before I died, I was having dreams of a man with a staff that he carried and a woman in a black hooded robe."

"You can see her blonde hair and blue eyes, blood on her chin." They both say at the same time, looking wide eyed at each other.

"So, there is some kind of purpose to this. How long ago was my funeral? Yesterday?"

"Grandpa, you died almost a year ago. I am just now coming to the estate for the first time since your funeral." I look at my grandfather with sadness on my face. "I have missed you every day since you died."

"I guess our concept of time does not exist here. I did not realize it has been a year already my dear boy." He gives me a sympathetic look.

"We better get to analyzing that book my boy. We have secrets to uncover, treasures of our past to be found." My grandfather was as giddy as a schoolboy, even for a dead schoolboy.

The white gloves go back on as I open the book. The book of secrets, at this point in time. I look at the first couple pages. My grandfather reads behind me, over my shoulder. The hairs on the back of his neck stand at attention, a chill runs down my spine. My response is to shiver.

"Sorry my boy. I suppose I have that effect on you now. Do not want to distract you." He chuckles as he glides away, even though his motions look like he is walking.

The book starts off with the wizard Elzabus talking about his family, with a tree drawn, names of family. His family tree went back to his great grandparents. All of the Celtic Vikings descent. His family had come from a long lineage of magick.

"I suppose this Azalea that he has referred to is not related. There is no mention of her on the 'family tree.' She must have been someone that he knew from the village he lived in. It appears that every generation has had only a boy child. No girls have been born in the family for many centuries." I look over the family tree one more time as my grandfather stands there looking as if he is concentrating.

"Come to think of it, I do not recall having seen any girls births in my ancestry I completed. That is strange."

Sitting back in the chair, thinking about what they had just discovered with the family tree. A breeze blows through the library making the pages move in the book. A shiver once again travels down my spine.

Sitting forward to look into the book, I discover passages written about the village that Elzabus resided in. During his time there, he meets a young woman by the name of Azalea. She is immensely powerful according to him. He takes her under his wing as an apprentice of sorts. The period did not recognize women as being powerful, only as witches.

He writes about the amount of magic and power that this Azalea holds. She is not aware of the amount of power that she has, she is completely oblivious. He states that he feels guilty that he has to keep the truth from her. She is probably more powerful than Elzabus himself.

The next passages speak about a premonition Elzabus has that the village and castle were to be invaded by king Carazus. He was searching for

Elzabus to become the wizard of his castle. Elzabus had turned down the king's offer. The king did not take kindly to being refused. He left the village with his pregnant wife in hopes of deterring Carazus from attacking the village.

When Elzabus returned, he found all of the villagers, the duke and duchess slain. The sole survivor of the carnage was Azalea. Somehow, some way she had survived.

Turning the page came quickly as I was obsessed by the information now. I feel some kind of pull to know more about Azalea.

The story continues that Elzabus returned right after the slaughter. He witnessed Azalea holding her beloved Thomas in her arms. They were to be married in about a month.

The screams of pain from Azalea were heard from the distance Elzabus was from the castle walls. Her petite form rose from her spot to reach down to her father that lay an arm's length from her as well. The area around her vibrated with the magic that fought to be released as a hooded form, resembling the God Arawn approached her. Her magic strong enough to call forth the Gods themselves. Only the strongest of witches or wizards had the ability to do such things. A boom echoed through the air with the answer of God Arawn.

The vibrations of her magic could be felt by Elzabus. He tried to call out to her. She was deaf to his words. He watched as Azalea drank blood from Arawn to change into a creature like the Dearg Due. Her long blonde hair blew in the breeze as the magic swirled around her. Her darkness evident as the clouds descended upon the castle area. Wind blew, rain fell, and lightning struck the entire area.

The brightness of the lightning made him look away with the burning of his eyes, the stench of the burning flesh singed his nostrils, the cold settled into his bones with a fear he had never felt.

Elzabus returned to the king to take his place as his wizard. The king used his powers to conquer many kingdoms.

Word had spread of the Dearg due that plagued the area, killing every man she came across. The anniversary of the slaughter of his village and all who lived there was also the twenty-first birthday and inauguration of the kings son Vincent, as the new king.

Elzobus speaks of the premonition of the Dearg due taking the life of the new king, Vincent. He did not notify anyone of his vision of the death. The king and his son were both tyrants, with Vincent worse than his father. The world would suffer at the hands of Vincent if he were to live.

So, the vision came to pass of the death of King Vincent per the hands of the Dearg due, that Elzabus knew as Azalea. She was the servant of the 'soul-eater God, Arawn.'

Chapter 7

Sterling: Destination Known

Packing in a rush to get back on the plane to Ireland once again. I decide to attempt to summon my grandfather to go with me to Ireland. We found that my grandfather is now connected to me. My grandfather will now go where I go. Not sure whether I think that is a curse or a blessing at this time.

It became evident that no one other than myself can see or hear my grandfather besides myself. I made a deal with my grandfather to not cause me to talk to him or even look in his direction for fear of people thinking I was insane.

Money is not an issue as we exited the plane to have the limo take us to the hotel. The town is near where the village had been presumed to be located. The rubble of the castle remained. Mostly laying on the ground, some of the castle remained standing strong.

After making sure the unsavory guide had his money, we returned to the hotel room for the night. My grandfather and I were curious if the magic of our ancestors trickled down the branches to us.

I read a spell out to start a fire. I prepared the fireplace in the hotel room, starting the spell as it was written in the book. I spoke the words while I held my hand over the wood in the fireplace, to have it start burning. I felt the heat of the flame on my palm with the flames licking at my skin.

I climbed into bed as my grandfather read the pages that were open of the spells. He would be able to complete the spells hopefully just as well as myself. Being dead may cause an issue with performing the spells though. Otherwise, he could recite the words to me to mimic, casting the spells.

I look to my red hands, covered in blood. I have no idea where the blood is coming from. Is this even my own blood? Where is grandfather? I need to find out what is going on. I look around to not recognize any of my surroundings. Where am I? I am outside, on the forest floor, surrounded by pines and numerous dead knights and soldiers alike.

I watch as the beautiful Azalea is talking to the wizard Elzabus. Her long blonde hair shimmers in the moonlight that peeks through the tops of the pines. No other sounds around besides the sweet melody of her voice. I could listen to her talk all of the time.

I see a tear fall from her blue eye, which was once red as blood. She lowers her blade from the wizards throat. She disappears into an opening in the ground to come out a few minutes later, as Elzabus remains in his place. The other part of the army will be here any minute since the others have not returned.

I have pain in my stomach. I put my hand over the pain to feel the warm sticky blood oozing from my stomach. Azalea had killed me. I remember that now. I do not blame her; we are here to take her back to the castle so Carazus can torture and kill her.

Azalea returns to Elzabus' side. They start to move up the mountainside. I follow them out of curiosity. Wait, I am dead. How am I still here? Oh yeah, she drank my blood.

The legends speak that if Azalea is to drink your blood and leave one drop before you die, the soul-eater comes for you. This time he is not here, so he cannot take me or my soul away. I gather with the other spirits that are circling above their heads.

Elzabus nearly lost his footing to plummet to his death a couple of times. I see Azalea reach out, grabbing him from harm's way each time.

Why exactly am I watching them from as distance? Why am I following her? I watch closely as she maneuvers up the mountain side.

They are closer to the top of the mountain. They reach a ledge with an accessible area. The wizard is speaking something as I see the mountainside open up to a room. I can see the ledge from where I am. I have no idea where I am though. I am now part of the sluagh that holds Azalea to the wizard and the area.

I sit up in the bed abruptly, looking around in a near panic. The sweat is beaded on my forehead, as I struggle to slow my breathing and heartbeat. The sheets are wet around my body. "I guess that is my cue to get in the shower right away." My grandfather pops his head from around the corner, scaring the shit out of me.

"That is not cool grandpa. I have had to deal with the fact that you had died a year ago and now you are scaring the shit out of me. What did I ever do to have this kind of punishment? Who did I piss off along the way?" I flop across the bed once again with a huff.

Grandpa Sterling moves to the edge of the bed to look down upon my face. "So, are you going to lay here all day?"

"I had the weirdest dream. Maybe you will understand it. I was watching Azalea with the wizard; they went up the side of the mountain to a place on a ledge area. I was part of what I knew was called the sluagh. She had killed me in my dream. I remember the feel of the blood on my hands. The blood was so warm, sticky, and thick on the palm of my hand."

Before I could say another word, my grandfather is up in my face, nearly touching me. The chill of the temperature dropping made a shiver run down my spine. "Whoa, whoa, whoa." He pauses, standing there just looking at me. "You mean to tell me that you are having visions of Azalea and the wizard. Were you thinking that you should not tell me about this, like it means nothing?"

"I am telling you about it right now, slow down grandpa. I just woke up from that dream. I have not had the opportunity or time to process the information. That is the entire gist of my dream. I had only good feelings toward Azalea, even though she had killed me. I thought her voice sounded heavenly to my ears."

"Do you think you might remember the mountainside and ledge area you saw in the dream?" Grandpa Sterling has a half grin on his face. The apparition of my grandfather is just not the same thing as him being there in 'the flesh,' so to speak. He still has the same sense of humor though.

"I think I would, but things have changed over the last 1,500 years some, I'm sure." I state this to him with eyes wide. "I will do my best to try and remember

73

everything I saw in the dream, or vision as you call it. If anything looks familiar, I will let you know.

Our unsavory guide is sitting outside of the hotel in a black SUV, waiting for me to come out. I have been waiting on him as I ate my breakfast, a fry-up, is what the Irish refer to as breakfast. The only thing I really cannot stomach is the black pudding, otherwise known as blood pudding.

The ride back to the rubble of a castle was quiet and long. The road is rough going, and the rain keeps coming down in a drizzle.

"You do have a crew waiting there for us, right? That was part of our agreement, and for what I paid you." The look must have been that of disbelief that I was giving him. He snapped his head over toward me, looking all kinds of pissed off.

"Do ye not trust me?" He wobbles his head. "Thinkin I am just going to take your money." The brisk stop of the head wobbled at me.

Grandpa Sterling sits there in the back seat of the SUV responding to every word and head shake the man makes. I thank whatever god is responsible for giving me the willpower to not laugh at my grandfather. My grandfather is sitting back behind him doing the same actions with his head, exaggerated movement of his arms, and acting totally absurd, just like the unsavory character that I was told I could trust.

The SUV comes to a halt after splashing through a huge mud puddle. Henry is seething, thinking that I am laughing at him. A couple of chuckles made it out of my mouth, clearing my throat afterward. It did not cover the laugh at all like I hoped it would. "Hey dude, I am not laughing at you." I was being honest about that. I was laughing at my grandfather.

I stepped out of the SUV for my grandfather waiting on me. "For the love of God, will you please stop making me laugh. They are going to run away screaming, thinking I am a lunatic on the loose.

Chapter 8

Sterling: The Discovery

The castle lay in rubble that had once been a glorious sight. The Duke and Duchess were the kindest of people, in the research I had read. Not a soul needed for anything within their area. The walls that once stood there, have only a few stones leading a path around the outer edge of the rubble.

I stumble, falling to the ground with my forehead hitting a rock. The guide and several other men run to the aid of myself sitting there rubbing my head to alleviate some of the stabbing pain. Someone provided me with ice. The goose egg on my head reminded me of how slippery the mud is.

It was as if someone flipped a switch in my mind. All of a sudden, I jump up to my feet , turning to the direction to the north of the castle remains. The mountains in the background, to the north are jagged and covered in rocks. The other mountainsides are covered in thick pine forests. The castle had set in a valley of sorts. A small opening in the pine trees comes into sight at the base of the mountain. An ancient fireplace made of stone, withstood the tests of time as it had some protection in the trees. Everyone decided that they would set up camp for the night here at the fireplace.

The pines surrounding the area made it seem that night is upon us. A trick of the eye as the sun setting peeked through the tops of the trees with a stiff breeze.

The tents are set up, with mine set up close to the fireplace as I requested. I had the feeling I was not alone, not just with grandfather either. Someone is watching me, waiting, for what I did not want to know. The night was not officially upon us as the fire is blazing in the pit.

Most of the crew sits by the fire in their folding chairs. They talk amung themselves. The sounds of the forest creatures would catch their attention occasionally. An owl let out a hoot as it swoops past the edge of the camp. Many of the men for the crew had grown up in this area. They knew many stories of the Dearg Due. Some of the men said it was only a fairy tale to scare the children into staying in the house during the night and others believed in the legends.

The guide spoke of the recent events that it is believed by the villagers in the area that the Dearg Due is back in the area. Several men have been found recently with all of the blood drained from their bodies without any explanation.

One of the men starts the story of the legend of the Dearg Due. The campfire roared as he began the story of the first woman vampire; at least known as that to the modern day person.

"The Dearg Due was a woman of undeniable beauty. She had blonde hair like the sun, with eyes as blue as the sky. She had a lover she was planning on getting married to within the month. Her beloved was murdered, leaving her to scream to the heavens with pain and seeking revenge."

"Her revenge came as the curse to kill any man she saw fit and she was also to do the bidding of the God Arawn, of the Underground and Death. He was known as a soul-eater. Lord Arawn was the god that heard the cries of pain from Azalea that fateful day." I shifted uncomfortably in my seat at the story. I knew of some of the story, but not all of it. My family had always talked about Elzabus, not Azalea.

"Azalea was created by the God Arawn. She drank of his blood in exchange for revenge on her lovers murderer, the king Carazus. With her now curse, she would need mortal blood to survive. She was to leave the last drop of blood in the man so that Arawn could have their last drop of blood and their soul."

"Azaleas curse made her immortal to do the bidding of Arawn for as long as he wanted her to do his deeds. The agreement was that Azalea would kill whom the Lord Arawn told her to. With her immortality, blood was needed for survival; she would be a creature of the night. She had the hearing and instincts of a creature of the night. The strength filled her of one-hundred men. She had learned to use her sword from a young age, making her very talented. She trained with many knights." Henry takes a drink of his bottle of beer as the fire pops loudly. Visibly every man listening to the story, jumps.

"She always waited for her chance to kill the king. She was never told by Arawn that it was her turn for revenge. Azalea disappeared off the face of the planet. King Carazus and the Lord Arawn searched for her for years. She was never to be found. As far as anyone knows, she is dead. There have been random cases of men dying of mysterious circumstances, never to be questioned. It was said that Lord Arawn was demanding and had become selfish with Azalea giving him the souls that he had wanted, so he created more creatures such as Azalea to satiate his taste for mortal souls."

"Nothing of course has ever been proven that these creatures we now refer to as 'vampires', exist. People tend to look the other way when there is something that they cannot explain."

"She never did get her revenge?" I asked the question, but somehow I know that she still had a soul left.

"The deal was for him to have her soul after she completed, exacted her revenge on the king."

Henry gets up from his chair. "I am going to go in to sleep now. Good luck sleeping tonight. See you all in the morning hopefully."

"You are such as asshole," several of the men yell to him. Empty cans pelt him from across the fire. His wicked laugh continues as he finally enters his tent. The fire is only burning coals. No strong winds to carry embers to start a fire.

I decide to call it a night. The remaining embers casts an ominous glow into the tent. Shadows dance around the sides of the tent. The stories told tonight made a sadness settle into my soul for Azalea. The haunting images of the beautiful woman sitting alone crying seemed to break my heart.

The warm soft body beneath my own calls to me for more. I pull my head back to look into the pools of blue. The blonde hair like a halo around her head. She smiles up to me with a giggle.

The pelt on the ground beneath us, warm and soft. My hand traces the side of her face to her neckline, caressing over her collarbone. Her skin so soft and creamy white. She rolls her head to the side as I trace down her chest. The feel of her body responding to mine causes a tingle to run the length of my spine.

Her naked breasts against my bare chest, rubbing with each breath she takes. I can't resist the red lips, as I press mine against hers. She kisses me with passion we both feel. She arches her back to push into me more. My needs grow more with each second as I lose control of my body with the need to feel myself buried deep within her.

81

"Are you ready for me again my love? I want you again so much. I cannot seem to get enough of you. My hand travels down her side with the tips of my fingers to trace along her hip bone, to her core. She is wet and ready for me, as she moans with my touch. I gently rub the area knowing she is swollen from making love to me already.

I position between her thighs, pushing against her opening as she bites my earlobe. I groan as she whispers to me, "take me Sterling, take me now. I want you inside of me again and again." I push into her hot wet core slowly, to savor in the tightness. The feeling of being inside of her nearly pushes me to the brink of insanity as I breathe in to control my body, my soul, and my mind. Lowering my head for my lips to meet with hers, I feel a tooth pierce my lip. The trickle of blood from my lip touches her tongue, a moan escapes her.

I wake up slowly, with the memories of the dream lingering. It, of course, is at that moment my mind decides to recognize the fact that she just spoke my name of Sterling. I am not dreaming but having a vision of a future event. My body screams for her, my mind thinks of only her, I know I must find her.

I awoke with the most painful erection of my life. I can still see her as I close my eyes. Sitting up to relieve some of the pressure, doesn't help. A dip in the cool river nearby would be the trick. The suns rays are just peeking over the horizon with rays of pinks and oranges. The rain clouds gone for now. It is a beautiful morning.

Just as I am getting out of he river, I am joined by some other men who have the same idea for the start to the morning.

Something inside of me says that today is the day that we finds answers. The answers to which questions though. Speaking of which, I have not seen my grandfather this morning yet. Either that states he has been losing his mind with hallucinations or grandpa is up to some shenanigans. I know him all too well.

Just as that fleeting thought passes, grandfather appears around the corner, nearly giving me a heart attack of my own. "For the love of god, stop doing that. You are going to kill me." I hold my chest to emphasize the statement. "You know, I am not exactly a spring chicken any longer grandfather." Letting out a laugh at my statement.

"By the way. I almost forgot to tell you that I had another vision with Azalea." I knew that would get grandfather all worked up.

"You had another vision last night and you have not told me about it yet?" His eyes wide with a look of shock on his face.

"Nothing to worry about really. It must have been as fantasy or wet dream." I chuckle while watching grandfather look at me sideways. His lips pucker into a scowl. "My dream had to do with sex grandpa. I dreamed of having sex with Azalea. It did seem very real though."

"Was there anything about it that makes you think it may have been a vision and not just a dream?" he looks at me as if he is looking over glasses, one brow up, warning me to answer without joking around. He is showing me that he is serious.

I thought about the dream again. I am not starting to lose the details of the dream yet. "Maybe there is something to the fact that I am not forgetting the details of the dream and I do remember, she called me by my name. She said Sterling." I tilt my head in realization of that. "That is a bit odd." I mumble to myself.

The guide tosses me a backpack for the hike up the mountain. "We need to be careful up there. There are many ways for you to slip and die. Go slowly and make sound decisions. If you feel it is time to stop and dig, you need to yell out to me. I will lead with you directly behind me."

As we all start to climb the mountainside I can feel my guts twist and turn. I have the butterflies in my stomach too. "Since when does Sterling Mason get the butterflies?" I laugh to myself with the mumbling of my words. The pull up the hill is giving me the strength to go on faster.

The guide has to ask me to slow down for all of the others to catch up. The men need a break from the elevation change. I realize I need a break as well. My fingertips come over the ledge of the area just above to rest. The second my fingertips touch the ledge a jolt of electricity travels the length of my body. The visible shiver has the attention of my grandfather. "We are close my boy. I know you can feel it too."

Standing on the ledge, there was enough room for everyone to make it to the spot safely. I stood there looking at the side of the mountain. "This place here is

85

where we will start. Set up the area for the dig to start in the morning."

The retreat back down the mountain is much easier than the climb up. The pull to return to the ledge was so much, that I nearly turned around several times. The sun is on the horizon as we enter the camp. The sunset promises for another amazing night under the stars, that we can see through the thick pines.

I am restless as I am out pacing around the tent, contemplating everything in life at this time. The thoughts of grandfather actually being with him first of all. I speak aloud as I pace. "Since when are there ghosts or spirits? I have never believed or disbelieved in them, just never thought about it I suppose. There has never been a reason to think about the apparition of my grandfather haunting me someday to finish what he had started, so many years ago."

The chill of my grandfather beside me, draws my attention. I stop to look at my grandfather for a moment as he points down at the ground. A metal pull handle protrudes from the ground just slightly. I kneel beside it to clear the earth from around the metal handle. The layer of moss and dirt cover a square piece of wood. I yell for some of the guys to come help him with the project that is now underway.

Torches are set up around the area as the darkness has fallen over the camp. The torches cast enough of a glow to see that the metal handle is that of a door, a door into the ground.

After the area had been cleared the team went about opening the door as carefully as possible to not disturb anything that may be under it. A large slab of material is shoved under the door to the opposite edge. The door is carefully moved from its spot.

The door opens to an area dug out of the ground resembling a small cave. The dirt had filtered in around the door over the years of laying in wait to be found. Nothing is in the small room as a light is lowered into the cave. Disappointment washes over me as I am hoping to find something today. The shadows of the light reveal that there is a tunnel off of the small room.

I lower myself into the small cave to follow the path of the tunnel. Men walk above in the direction they are told the tunnel is going. When I reach the end of the tunnel it is closed off. The men outside start to dig the area that is to become the opening of the tunnel.

There had obviously been a home here with a small escape room with a tunnel. Only wizards, witches and exhiled people lived alone in the woods. There is a spark of hope that he may find some evidence of Elzabus or Azalea around here yet.

Chapter 9

Finding Azalea

Excitement courses through the men as the opening of the tunnel collapses in the rest of the way. I cough a couple times and wave my hand in front of my face, to fan the dirt away.

I have a hand extended to me to assist me out of the tunnel. I stand at the opening of the tunnel as something takes over my mind. I feel my body stiffen and jerk like a seizure as I have flashbacks of the vision of Azalea and Elzabus. I rewatch the entire scene replaying in my head again of Azalea holding a knife to his throat, putting it down, disappearing into the tunnel I now know, and leaving to go up the side of the mountain.

I open my eyes to the sound of my name and a stinging to my face. I sit up shaking my head, clearing the sting of my skin and the vision.

"What the hell happened to you back there? We were all standing there when you decided to have a seizure or something. You fell to the ground, staring into space." Henry had a look of concern on his face for me.

"I will be fine Henry. I must have gotten overwhelmed and with the elevation changes is all." I thought it sounded like a good excuse.

"If you say so. Don't take offense to the slap." Henry huffed before he walked away, looking back over his shoulder at me.

I was up most of the night. I could not sleep knowing that today I was going to find something with Azalea. The excitement was near maddening. Every nerve ending in my body tingled with anticipation for the moment that we found something. Now I realize why grandfather was acting as he had been before we left home.

The morning light sent beams of glorious sun over the mountains. No rain clouds. Two complete days now without any rain. The mud puddles have all dried up and the ground no longer soggy.

The men moved quickly to get ready to head up the mountain in search of more discoveries. Everyone in camp was ready quicker than usual. Finding the cave and tunnel provided the inspiration to light a fire under the asses of the men that now believe there is something out there.

My mind is a muddled mess as I climb the mountainside. The memories of the visions invade my mind like the plague that will either be my salvation or possibly my demise. Grandfather is talking to me, but I don't hear his words as I am in my own world.

Grandfather knows exactly how to get my attention as he touches me. The chill runs down my spine, bringing my attention back to what I was doing and to listening to what grandfather has to say.

The same feeling of an odd pull comes over me as I climb onto the ledge. The vision once again takes over my body and mind as I approach a spot, moving rocks and clawing at the dirt with my bare hands.

Henry stops me with a hand to my shoulder. "We have tools for that Sterling. Let us start our jobs. Why you paid us."

I step back as the vision of looking out at the sky behind me. I turn to see Elzabus looking over the ledge to plummet to his death. He was escaping from the king's army that was approaching. "What is happening my boy?"

I start speaking aloud for all to hear what I see through the vision that has taken over my mind. Some of the men and Henry look to me with fascination as I continue to tell them what I had just seen. The men continue to move the rocks and dirt away from the spot I designated.

The rocks and dirt start to fall inward to an open space. "You may be right about this spot Sterling. There is an opening behind these rocks."

I feel an immediate urge to get into the opening behind the rocks. The sun's rays seemed to shine directly onto the spot of the dig. The last of the rocks are moved as the clouds form to cover the sun. The sun is now completely crowded as angry billowing clouds form in the distance. I grab my flashlight to head into the unknown. I know from the visions that Azalea was left in this cave by Elzabus for her safe keeping. If the legends are true. She will be in the small cave, sleeping as if death had taken her, but preserved her body.

"Henry, I want you to pay the men double their wage to get them to not speak of this to another soul. We found nothing. They can leave now. I need to be alone now."

"Are you sure about that Sterling? The men would like to know what they have helped you to find. We can help you, but if you wish it, we will leave immediately."

"Thank you, Henry for all of your help. I have it from here. Please leave my tent set up for me. I may stay another night."

The flashlight provided just enough light to see inside of the cave. Grandfather had gone in first to make sure it was safe for me to go in. He yelled for me with such excitement that I literally ran into the cave. He could only go into the cave so far due to the magic that held him away.

Laying there on a bed of furs is the most beautiful woman I have ever laid my eyes on. I knew immediately that the woman was Azalea. It was the exact description of her everywhere he had read and every vision he had had of her.

Time seems to stand still. The sleepless nights of searching, wondering, and dreaming about Azalea. Here she lays in front of my very eyes. She isn't moving or even breathing is what it looks like.

The winds blew as the clouds formed to cover what is left of the setting sun. I watch from the ledge of the mountainside. I would have to wait until morning to get her down the side of the mountain.

I feel the air become cooler as it makes me shiver from my head to my toes. The type of chill that hits the nerves of the bone. I take a deep breath and stretch my body to clear the chill from my mind and body. The air seems thick and heavy with something that grips your heart, squeezing like death is in the air. I start to wonder if we have done the right thing. A little too late now.

I close my eyes to feel the last of the warmth of the sun wash over my body. The stillness of any other sounds confuses me. I tilt my head to listen for any signs of life besides the beat of my heart.

Chapter 10

Azalea Awakens

Sterling enters the cave once again to look upon Azalea. How could such a beautiful creature be called a monster? Her skin smooth and milky white, her lips red, with blond hair like a halo.

Once again, he turns to look at the storm brewing outside. The clouds seemed to move in an odd pattern. It was not any particular pattern, random, but moving. "Well, that is definitely interesting. Is that actually a flock of birds? What is that?" He squints to focus more.

"That is a murder of crows that I am looking at." They pelt the opening of the cave without entering. They attempt to enter again as a human form without success. "I must be imagining shit now. I don't know how much more of the odd and mysterious I can take. Ghosts, vampires, and now a murder of crows making the form of a human."

"Are you talking about me? Your voice woke me." He turns around so fast that he stumbles, landing against the wall, looking at Azalea standing before him. "Don't go out there right now. You will be possessed and by what, I have no idea. Who are you? Why are you here? You realize I will kill you?"

She watches as the mortal has wide eyes, looking at her with confusion and surprise written all over his face. His skin turns pale to almost a green color. "You are going to pass out now, aren't you?"

In a set of quick movements, she catches the solid body of a man that smelled amazing and warm. She laid him on the furs, waiting impatiently for a couple of minutes before she started to tap his cheeks. She feels a weakness take over her body. "How long have I been sleeping? I need answers, but I need blood first and foremost."

Sterling opens his eyes to look up at Azalea. She holds herself over his body, looking into his amber-yellow eyes, full of something other than fear. Her hair hangs around their faces like a sheer veil.

She whispers against his lips to move along his jaw to his ear lobe. "So, who is in control? I am meaner than your demons can ever be. I would make your demons weep. You should be scared of me."

Her tongue traces the outer shell of his ear to feel his body shudder beneath her. The pleasure of the control she has over this man's body is different than any other man. Why is he so different?

She feels a wave of weakness roll through her body. Her head rolls back as her teeth protrude watching his carotid artery thump in his neck.

In her weakness he is able to roll her off of his body. She lays on the dirt floor, looking up to the man that is so different. The weakness increases more with each moment.

Sterling stands with his back against the wall. "Were you going to eat me? Really? I find you, free you and you try to kill me. This supernatural shit is really starting to piss me off." He watches as the beautiful creature in front of him is dying of hunger, literally.

"If I let you have some blood, do you promise to not kill me?" He stands there with a brow raised, waiting for a reply.

"I promise." She barely has the strength to choke out the words to him.

Sterling approaches Azalea slowly, cautiously. He drops to his knees next to Azalea. He looks around to find that she has a dagger in a belt on her hip. The blade glimmered in the light of the lantern. A flash of light makes Sterling reflect on all that is happening in his life. No time right now to think. I need to act. For some reason, I need to save her.

He runs the blade of the dagger from his wrist toward his inner elbow, making about a three-inch cut that blood immediately oozes from. Gritting his teeth as the blade stung like a fire to his arm. He puts his arm over the red lips of Azalea. She opens her lips to have the drops of blood enter her mouth.

Sterling moves closer as she wraps her elegant fingers around his forearm. He lays her head in his lap as she drinks the blood coming from the open wound. He starts to feel somewhat dizzy. "You need to stop Azalea. You are going to take too much. You promised." He pulls his arm away or she releases it, one or the other. He scoots himself until he is sitting against the wall.

As Azalea removes her mouth, the wound immediately starts to heal, and there isn't any pain. The cut is such a small spot that you would never know a cut had been there.

"Thank you. I needed that. You are absolutely delicious. You see my dear. That is how I feed on the mortals. I need to do some catching up I feel. May I do something?"

"I can't spare anymore blood right now Azalea."

"I am not asking for that. I think I have been locked in my personal prison for way too long. I can read your mind and catch up on the time I have lost."

"That would be fine."

Azalea sits in front of Sterling, looking into his eyes. He wanted so badly to touch her and feel her lips on his own. No matter whether she just drank his blood or not.

She picks up his hand, placing it on her cheek. He runs his thumb over her bottom lip as she closes her eyes to the feel of his touch. She had never enjoyed the feel of any man, other than Thomas. This man is different for some reason. She leans forward, touching her lips to his. Her tongue comes out to touch his lips as he realizes what is happening. He pulls back in surprise.

"I'm so sorry Azalea. I had no right to touch you like that." He continued to look into her blue eyes as she placed both of her hands over his temples, looking into his eyes.

"Nothing to be sorry about. I heard your needs, and I was happy to oblige you. I rather enjoyed it. I am not an innocent. By the way, what is your name?"

The thought had not occurred to him that he had never told her his name. "My name is Sterling Thomas Mason. I know who you are. You are Azalea."

"I am Azalea Suzanne Getta. My fiancé's name was Thomas. That is so odd that you have the same name." She continues to hold his head in the palms of her hands.

Sterling became lost in Azalea's eyes. The sea of blue sucked him into thoughts of the ocean, the skies on a clear summer day.

He envisions himself laying in the grass with Azalea at his side. He looks over to her smiling face. She is so beautiful. Nothing on the earth can compare to her beauty. The Gods themselves would revel in her beauty. At that thought the blue skies turn to a gray with crows filling the skies.

A tall dark human-like form approaches from the edge of the ocean. The shadows follow in his path. I just know the form is a male. Must be with the way that he is walking or carrying himself. The arrogance in his movements make Sterling cringe. This form has to be the God Arawn he had read about in the history books.

As he gets closer to Sterling, a shiver crawls down his spine like the slithering of a snake. The air becomes heavy and insufferably difficult to inhale. The smell of the mortar and sulfur surrounds the area making his stomach churn.

Azalea no longer lay beside him in the grass. Instead of being next to him he sees her step from behind Arawn, to standing beside him. Her black leather on with a black hooded robe, pulled down over her eyes, causing a shadow to cover her beauty. Her mouth open, her teeth long and sharp as she screams

loud enough for me to drop to my knees, holding my
ears.

Chapter 11

Getting to Know You

The ground shakes as her scream continues. All that stood in the way, fell to the ground in agonizing pain. Stepping from behind her are several more men and women, all of whom have long sharp teeth. Every one of the people around her have silver eyes that look like the reflection of the moons rays on a blade.

Azalea puts her hand up, as every one of the other vampires kneel at her feet. Azalea stands in place as if she were a Goddess herself. A set of boney hands appear from behind her to place a crown upon her head by Arawn, that then bowed to her. "Queen Azalea of the Underworld."

Just like that, the vision was gone just as quickly as it appeared. He opens his eyes to have Azalea staring at him.

"What was that? You are having premonitions. You are filled with magic." She reached toward him again to watch as the arc of electricity jumped out connecting to him. The electricity literally sizzled between them as they sat there on the cave floor. Her fingertips nearly touched his outstretched palm. They were both mesmerized, watching intently, tilting their heads as she moved her hand around his. His hand shifted slightly as he laced his fingers with hers.

The sudden jolt of electricity between them causes them to both take a breath. Before he knew what was happening, Azalea is sitting on his lap, legs wrapped around his waist. Her lips crush down on his in a fury of electricity invading their bodies in pulses.

"You, are, Thomas." She states, pulling her head back slightly. "At least the reincarnation of him. We are meant to be together," she speaks breathlessly.

He is in no state to argue with her as his pants tighten more with the kiss, her body rubbing on his. It is like something feral takes over his body. A hunger unlike anything he had ever felt before, washes over his body in waves of pulsing.

His hands came up to grab two hands full of hair. Her head went back as his mouth descended upon her neck. Her pulse point pounding harder by the moment. Her hands tangle in the back of his hair as a moan escapes her. Every sense is now filled with and activated by them, there, in this position. Her pelvis moves over his sensually, grinding and circling.

"Take me now. I need you."

The only words that Sterling needed to hear as he stood, taking her to the furs. The feral feeling of raw sexual emotion continued to flow through their bodies. The ache that Azalea had for Sterling was too much for her to handle as she flips them over in a mere movement to sit atop of Sterling. She rips his shirt open for the buttons to pop in all directions.

She stood up over the top of Sterling as all he could do was watch in awe at the beauty of her. She undid her pants just as quickly with them off in an instant.

"I guess we don't need all of the four-play anyway." He chuckles aloud as she looks down at him with dark eyes. The lust taking over all sense of reality as his pants come undone.

Before he can think, she has her hand wrapped around him, covering the head with her hot wet mouth. The fulmination of a feeling of satisfaction hummed through his body as she continues to use her tongue to torture him. A low groan emanates from his chest.

"I think you might be ready. I know I am. I have waited what seems like forever to feel your touch and make love to you once again."

Azalea goes from standing over him to kneeling, she takes her clothes off. She once again claimed his mouth with a passion he had never felt before.

She straddles his body, settling her body over and around his. They both moan as electricity tickles every part of their bodies that touch. She lays over his chest to increase the sensations. His hand travels up to the back of her head to fist his hand full of her blonde hair. Her moans of ecstasy nearly send him over the edge of the abyss as his other hand moves up her body slowly to circle his fingers around her throat, lightly squeezing as her hand covers his, encouraging his actions.

Their bodies form together into one, as the pit of her stomach uncoils just as his did. The explosion of feelings ignite the air around them, as if into flames. The fire of the venom runs through his veins from her bite once again to instantly diminish to pleasure.

She didn't drink his blood this time, so his body could produce more from his offering. The rush of adrenaline mixed with the orgasm was phenomenal for both of them.

Sterling needed to get some rest if he were to travel back down the mountain in the morning. Maybe the ravens would be gone by morning. He fell into a deep sleep as Azalea approached the opening in the side of the mountain, her prison of hundreds of years. Too many to count.

Azalea steps forward as the ravens form into the shape of a human. She performs a spell that encases the flock into a bubble. The sluagh spoke after another spell from Azalea. She had knowledge that she was not aware of from Sterling. A book of magic that had been Elzabus' would be ever so helpful now.

The sluagh screamed and screeched to be released. The malevolent spirits wanted their freedom from the prison they now inhabited.

"You will now pledge your loyalty to me. You will only take commands from myself. Lord Balor is no longer available to this world. Do you pledge loyalty to me now?" Azalea moves in a slow circle around the sluagh's prison with her arms crossed the entire time. She tapped her long fingers in a rhythm.

"We the sluagh pledge our loyalty to you, our queen. You are the Queen as appointed by Arawn many years ago. We will always be true to you." She stood there looking at the ground twisting her face as if she were debating the offer. She tapped one long, elegant finger over her lips.

"I will free you of your prison, but …. You will stay close to me. I will call upon you as I wish, for you to assist me. The man Sterling will be free of any harm from you as well. He is mine. You will protect him as if you were to protect me. Understand?"

"We understand our queen."

The bubble imprisoning the sluagh disappeared with the wave of her hand. She now needs to find the book that Elzabus created with spells and the history of king Carazus. She will have her day with the family of Carazus, just as he did with hers.

Sterling will awaken and we will go to the book.

Chapter 12

Azalea: Loyalties

Within a blink, we are at the base of the mountain again. I keep my arms wrapped around him as I inspect the area. "Now you know why I told you to keep your eyes closed. Otherwise, you will get sick and puke everywhere with the speed I can move at. "

The area is clear of any other humans. My strength is fading fast as I require more blood after such a long sleep and such vigorous activities with this mortal. There is definitely something special about him. Everything screams for me to drink his blood, yet I hesitate at the glowing of his golden eyes.

The camp had been cleaned up and cleared out as he had requested, except for his tent. We enter the tent as I am looking around at the artifacts that had been found during the dig. The first thing I notice is the set of swords that is now rusted and blackened with time and the elements.

I stop suddenly, waiting and listening. I close my eyes to focus. I hear another sound. Before Sterling has a moment to ask me what I hear, I am out of the door and out of sight. He pokes his head out of the door flap, looking around the area, eyes squinted. Finally, his eyes see a movement in the tree line. He holds his breath as he watches intently as Henry comes out of the bushes.

"What the hell are you still doing here? I thought everyone left."

"Everyone did leave. I had to come back. I knew that whatever you found had to be worth lots of money or else you wouldn't have sent us all away like you did. So, whatever are you keeping secret Sterling?"

"It isn't anything of money value. I paid you more than fairly for what you did. Now you should leave if you know what's good for you." Sterling turned away just as the knife Henry had been holding behind his back comes up to push into his neck.

"Big mistake, whoever you are. You don't touch what is mine." Is all that Sterling heard as the next sound is Henry's body hitting the ground in a pile. He dared not to turn around. He knew what he would see, and he didn't know if he was ready to see anything like that.

"Let us go for a walk before God Arawn arrives." I laced my arm around his as I directed him out of the tent without looking at Henry. It was too late to get away before Arawn made his entrance.

The darkness became darker. The human form made its way toward them. We stop in our places as he descends upon them. The black hood remains in place as his pale boney hand protrudes from the depths of the sleeve to cup Azalea's face momentarily.

"I have missed you, my dear queen. Where have you been hiding for all of these years? I searched for you for hundreds of years. I replaced you a hundred-fold over, without any comparison to you and your abilities. My queen has returned to me." His hand once again returned to the cheek of Azalea.

Arawn made a slow circle around them. His robe dragged but yet, somehow not dragging. The smoke and haze that followed him lingered. "I want you at my side in the Underworld as a Goddess, Azalea. The queen of blood and souls. Otherwise, I can claim my soul from you that you had agreed upon."

"You will not have my soul as I was never able to exact my revenge on Carazus as you promised in exchange. You did not fulfill your end of the bargain and therefore, there is nothing you can do about it. King Carazus has been dead and gone for more than a thousand years now."

My face turned dark with crimson eyes. My beautiful face was now unrecognizable. I pull my hood up slowly over my face as I push Sterling behind myself. "You will provide me with the satisfaction of his family members now. I need, I demand, satisfaction. Only when I have quenched my thirst for the blood of Carazus' family blood line, will I submit myself to you. If you try to make me stay now, the heavens will fall in rubble with the death of a god on the earth."

The dark skies seemed to take on a life of their own as the billowing clouds moved with purpose above. Sterling watched as the flock of birds that had been at the opening of the cave flew overhead. He realized after it was explained to him, that the sluagh had become devoted to me. They had pledged their loyalty to me.

Sterling knew with his education of the history that I was pretty much a force to be reckoned with now. The God Arawn has nothing over me now. I am stronger and have more power than any other being on the planet. In that moment, is when Sterling realized his grandfather would now be within the sluagh of spirits.

Only a spell from the book of Elzabus would be able to save him now. His spirit would have been pulled into the murder without question. The angry spirits were not choosy of the other spirits that occupied space with them. The book of spells was in the town now with Dirk, but he may have returned to the estate like they had agreed if he didn't return with Henry, or anything should happen. The book needed to be kept safe at all costs.

Sterling didn't think that the services of the airplane would be needed now. He was feeling pretty certain that they would make it back just fine.

The disturbing sounds of screaming and screeching filled the area. The sky remained dark as night. The shadows within the tree line began to move a slow dance of death, as they move along. It was as if Balor himself had emerged from the depths to move about one last time. The sluagh would have no choice but to obey their master, Balor, who included his grandfather.

Arawn sneered at me. "You will make an amazing goddess someday. I will be there to obtain my souls if you should need my assistance. I will speak more with you later, my queen. I will obtain my soul offering tonight and be on my way, for now." Moving quickly over Henry to obtain his last drop of blood and his soul.

Chapter 13

Sterling: The Estate

The trip back to the estate came after a spell. I closed my eyes and held my breath for the few moments it took to get to the estate. Even with my actions, I found myself sick. I ran to the grass along the cobblestone pathway to the house to heave my guts out as Azalea laughed.

The large wooden door of the estate opens to Betsy and Tim standing there in awe. Once they both gained their bearings, they knelt on one knee to Azalea as I look at them with confusion.

"We knew you would return to us with Azalea. We were hoping so anyway. Your grandfather never gave up on you finding her. Even after he died, he never lost his faith in you." Betsy bowed her head again as she realized what she had just said.

"You mean to tell me that you know about my grandfather, and you didn't tell me? You have been there throughout my entire life. I think I need to have all of this explained to me." I ran my hand through my hair as I took a deep breath in and let it out with a huff.

Betsy wrapped her aged arms around me in a warm, welcoming hug for my return. I had to lean down for her to reach around my neck. She motioned for me to lean down, like she always did. "I am so sorry my dear boy. We will talk more later. So, where is your grandfather?"

"That is a long story. I think he is in the sluagh that was holding Azalea. I know there was a spell in the book for this. I just have to get to the book. Dirk should have brought it back home." Azalea watched me closely as I mentioned the book of spells that she would need, to regain all of her powers back. Most of her magic was coming back to her with time passing.

Betsy and Tim welcomed them in with open arms. "We have adequate quarters set up for you Miss Azalea. Is that what you would like us to call you?" Betsy wrung her hands nervously as she waited patiently for an answer.

"I won't have you call me anything other than Azalea." She looked at all of the paintings that decorated the estates walls. She wandered, not even realizing where she was going, to end up opening the doors of the library.

Azalea stood in place holding her breath as she looked at the massive walls of books available. Her curiosity went back to the book. She scanned the area in search of the book.

Sterling stepped up behind Azalea frightening her. Her primary instinct made her react. She turned around at lightning speed to wrap her long fingers around my throat, lifting me until my feet were no longer on the floor. Her fangs protruded as her eyes turned a crimson. She was always on the alert. The one time she wasn't, and I happened to find it. She realized what she was doing, dropping me to the floor. She turned away from me quickly, to keep me from looking at her face.

The soft touch of my fingers to her shoulder seemed to calm her nerves from what had just happened. "I need you to promise me that you won't eat the help."

Azalea turned at breakneck speed, once again, to look at me covering my mouth, holding my laughter in. "Not funny Sterling. I only approach the people who are of the evil kind. I will have you know that I don't kill people either. It is Arawn that completes the life cycle, not me. I am not a killer, just because I am a monster." A sadness flashed in her eyes.

"I don't think you are a monster, no one here does." I stepped in closer to her, taking her face in my hands. I placed my lips a breath away from hers, while I looked deep into her eyes. "You are not a monster."

The kiss lingered for a few more moments before Betsy and Tim entered the room behind them. "I want you to make yourself at home. I need to go find Dirk and talk to him for a while."

I found Dirk in the basement with the book as he had been instructed to do. He needed to get his grandfather out of the sluagh that had followed Azalea to the estate now. Her protection from what, he had no idea.

Azalea met them as the sun was setting to summon her creature, the sluagh. The flock of birds that moved in unison through the trees as if they belonged there. Likely with my grandfather among them, he was part of that.

The blackness of the flock seemed more intimidating than it had been earlier. The vision of the wall of darkness approaching us. The screeching of the spirits and the sounds of the birds combined was enough to pierce your ears and crack your skull in pain.

Azalea stood in the open area with her arms out. She spoke a spell which Sterling was not familiar with. The spirit of his grandfather, rather the apparition of him moved away from the flock of birds. He was free of the sluagh once again. Azalea made it be so.

Grandfather Sterling notified us that it was his time to move along to the next part of the journey. He reaffirmed to us that eventually we would all be reunited again as we are reincarnated eventually.

I received some console from the fact that I would see my grandfather again sometime. The fact that there were even spirits into apparitions was enough to send his mind reeling. A completely new world has opened up to me.

Chapter 14

Azalea: Knowledge

The sounds of the night creatures had changed since I had last heard them. The bugs were noisier now. The bullfrogs sounded deeper. The air smelled different as the earth beneath my feet felt different. Nothing was as it had once been. I wasn't even in the same country.

Vampires is what they call the other creatures like me. I chuckled as I sat in the chair looking out of the open French doors to a lovely pond and flower garden. The small pond had a statue of a half-naked woman that resembled me. You would think it to be coincidence, but no witch believes in such things. Everything has a purpose or meaning. Sometimes you just have to look to find it.

A vision of Sterling came to me, of him lying on the cold hard floor. A single line of blood trickled from Sterling's head to a small pool. The red of the blood set me afire. The life-giving blood that he had freely given to me. I knew that I must find him. I had stayed in the library, reading every book that I could, to get familiar with humanity as it was now.

The sun had given way to the night. The moon full. No wonder the creatures were so loud. The fire raged from within me for the smell of his blood. The smell hit me immediately when I thought of him. The aroma strong enough that he had to be close.

I followed the smell of his blood and sound of his steady heartbeat. My senses keen and as sharp as the tips of my blades.

The smell of his blood led me through the house, to the basement stairs in the kitchen. The house was quiet. No one else was in the house that I could hear or sense. Where was everyone? I had gotten lost in the words of all of the books of the library, not noticing the changes going on around me. The chill started at the base of my spine, to travel up slowly to the base of my skull, causing a shiver to take over my muscles.

The only time I had had that feeling was with the presence of Arawn. That was not possible, but something was off. The smell of death lingered in the air. The smell of blood invaded me once again, clouding my thinking. This was not Sterling's blood.

119

Something else, someone else. The smell was familiar to me though.

The blanket came down over my head. My instincts demand that I jump away from the captor, successfully pulling the blanket off in the action. In the air I caught sight of the flash of silver eyes, fangs, and blood dripping from them.

The figure was gone before I landed back onto the cold concrete floor again. There was no denying that Arawn had been busy making more minions for himself in my absence. The question still remained of what had happened here. Sterling was still alive, but unconscious at the time.

A dagger in his hand as he had cut whoever had been there, the other vampire. My senses came alive even more as the smell of the blood, not just any blood. The smell of King Carazus' blood filled my sinuses as I brought the dagger to my mouth. The tip of my tongue came out to lick the crimson liquid from the blade.

I can feel my entire body stiffen as I start to have visions of the past. The vision of Carazus makes my teeth protrude. I watch the visions as I stand there in a daze, but with my eyes closed, stuck in the vision. One that I felt I was meant to see.

The vision of Elzabus and myself in the cave. Elzabus leaps over the edge of the mountainside as the soldiers approach. He leaps to his death to evade his own death, from helping me. My eyes open quickly for the vision to continue of King Carazus standing over the body of Elzabus.

The sound of coughing pulls me out of my vision. I want to return to my vision. There is some kind of significance to the vision of Carazus being there.

The basement started out as a concrete area that was a wine cellar. An area of the wine racks was pulled forward on one side, like a door on hinges. I looked to Sterling that had coughed but still not conscious.

I enter the door frame into an office area with crushed red velvet. Plush oversized leather furniture gather around the front of a large desk, like the one in the library. Behind the desk, a vault the size of the wall. The large square door is open. Inside the room are several glass cases with exhibits inside.

The one that catches her eye is the swords that belonged to her family. The ones they had found were not the real ones, obviously. What were those that they found? Is there more that Sterling has kept from me?

The anger of betrayal boiled in my mind and veins. I slammed my hand down, slicing through my arm on the glass for it to break. The sting of the cut runs the length of my arm; blood rushes from my arm as I grab it with my other hand to stop the blood loss. The metallic smell triggers my hunger. Thoughts of warm blood filling my mouth invades my mind. I immediately start the healing process as the wound closes itself as I watch.

An alarm starts to sound as the lights went out in the area. A set of bars slam shut at the opening as I grab the swords to sheath them. I had hid them at the small cabin so many years ago. Now they are back with me where they should be. I approach the bars just as Sterling is getting to the barred door.

"Are you going to explain all of this to me, or am I going to have to kill you too?" My eyes flash silver and crimson with fangs protruding.

"I didn't know about this room. I swear Azalea. I knew about the basement room, but not the room you are in. I can't get you out." Sterling covers his ears from the sound of the alarms going off.

I reach through the bars, pulling Sterling to me. The stream of blood runs down his forehead and cheek of his face. My tongue darts out to run along his cheek, cleaning the blood off as I hold the back of his head by his hair. Sterling notices my eyes are a cloudy silver as I stand there not looking at him but like; through him.

I blink again to have my teeth return to normal and my eyes blue, with the flashing of red with the alarms. "Stand back." I pull the bars apart slightly as I slide the barred door back to its original position. The alarms stop and the lights turn back on again.

"What happened to you Azalea? You looked like you were in a trance or something." Sterling put his hand over his head where the wound was.

"I have another power about which you didn't know. I know you tell me the truth though. I can read your thoughts and see the truth in your blood. The blood holds memory for so long. I can choose to ignore the visions or see them. If you had lied to me, you would be dead right now. We need to get your wound covered though. I need to feed."

Chapter 15

Azalea: The Truth Be Told

Sterling sat in the oversized chair with his ice pack held firmly to his head. The bleeding has stopped, now I can go near him without 'vamping out,' as Sterling called it. He is just lucky that I had learned to control my thirst over the years.

The first order of business is to find out more about what is going on with everyone being gone. Who's blood did the other vampire have on them? Were Betsy and Tim dead, or taken as leverage over Sterling? People knew his grandfather and knew he had money that he passed on to Sterling. It is a well-known fact that Dirk, Betsy, and Tim are like family to him. They have always been with the family.

"I need to go and feed. I feel the weakness coming over me. If I am going to go against another vampire, I need my strength. Truth be told, she needs some time alone. How ironic is that after 1500 years alone? The trip to the city is quick. The estate isn't far from the city.

Walking along the city streets is the easy part. If I had walked down the streets like this in my time, I would have been burned at the stake. Many other time frames this would have been unacceptable as well. The culture as it is now, is my type of culture. Society holds standards that many seem to want to break.

The part of town I seek is that of the living, lost souls. The living that really didn't know how to or want to live. The sad, the lonely, the addicts. I have my doubts about the type of blood that this part of society will harbor.

From between the walls of the buildings, lost souls lived and stayed. A flash of silver eyes catch my attention. The person with the silver eyes approaches slowly as I stop walking, standing in place, watching, listening, and feeling. I have never met anyone like me.

The other vampire came to about five feet in front of me before falling to his knee in front of me, head down. "My queen. We have heard of your coming. We never figured in a million years you would show up here. The others would like to meet you too."

I lower my head to scan the area. I look right to left then back again, listening for anything behind myself. I slowly take steps to the left until my back meets the wall. I wanted my back against the wall. No one can surprise attack me from this stance. The vampires, which equaled at least ten, all knelt in front of me.

"My Queen. We mean you no harm. You are our true queen. We humble ourselves before you as your servants." He looks back down.

"I need sustenance. Where can I go around here?"

"Let us show you, my queen." He stands, holding his hand out to me. I look around myself one more time before I put my hand in his. I pull up my hood with my other hand. The remainder of the vampires follow behind us.

"I am Darek, my queen. I would like to introduce you to the place made of dreams for a vampire. I am at your disposal or for your use, my queen. Must I admit that your beauty is mesmerizing."

The group rounds the corner of the alleyway to knock on the old metal doors. The sign above states, 'The Lounge.' A small peephole opens up. The silver look in the eyes says everything.

The door opens for Darek to step inside, still holding my hand. "My queen, welcome." A narrow hallway with stairs dimly lit opens up to a much larger room. This must have been a theatre in the past is what my recent knowledge tells me. The music fills the room. "I had heard of this rock music. I rather like how it makes my body feel." My body automatically moves to the beat.

Rows of couches and other furniture sit along the walls and into a circle around the bar area. With each person we pass, I see a flicker in their eyes or smell the metallic scent of life.

The need to feed grows within me as I pass all of the vampires that were feeding on humans. These humans sit there letting the vampires drink from them.

"The vampires will stop before they drink too much of their blood."

Darek notices my looks of curiosity. "They are what we call, 'donors' my queen. Most humans do not know about the vampires. The ones that do will let us drink their blood. Most of the time this is of a sexual nature. Most humans have only certain vampires they allow to drink from them during sex. The intimate act increases the pleasure if you have never experienced it." His half smile told me that he was indeed wanting me to possess his body.

I decided years ago that sex is for my pleasure. I would use it as I saw fit. The pleasure of the sex is what I sought. The sex I had with Sterling seemed to be different though.

The couch areas have curtains drawn around them for privacy if it is wanted. Darek sits down on the circular couch to pull me next to himself. As I sit down there are several donors and vampires that kneel down to me.

A man and woman both approach me wearing only enough to cover their important areas. The woman kneels between my knees, sensually running her hands up my thighs, spreading my legs wider as she moves her hands up. As the woman gets to the juncture of my thighs, she slides her hands back down my inner thighs. She puts her hands behind herself to untie the small amount of fabric that covers her nipples.

The woman grabs my hands, putting them on her breasts. The woman's head falls back as she leans in with her neck exposed, to let me sink my teeth into the flawless flesh that kneels before me, offering herself freely. The flames burn through my veins to feed on her. I watch as her pulse pounds at her pulse point with excitement. The rush of the warm blood fills my mouth.

I have never touched another woman in such a way, sexually. I rather enjoy the feel of her breasts in my hands. I run my other hand up to hold the woman's soft long hair. The feel of the silky hair and soft skin intrigues me as I pull away from drinking.

The woman's pulse speeds up, indicating she is done providing blood, but still providing the sex.

My lips connect to the woman's lips for a soft, discovery type of kiss that in turn brings my blood to a boil for this woman. The kiss deepens as she moans into my mouth, making a connection of our tongues. The exhilaration forces me to take the passionate kiss the woman so willingly gives and receives. My core pulses with anticipation of need.

I turn to the man sitting next to us that has been rubbing my breasts as he takes off my top. I stand to lower my pants as the woman seductively hooks her fingers around the leather. She kisses the backs and inner parts of my thighs. I nod to the man as he pulls his pants down exposing a throbbing cock.

Without any waiting I lower herself onto him with a moan. My head falls back as I enjoy the pleasure from the man and woman. The soft skin and hard nipples of the woman caress my back as her hand comes around to the front to rub my clit. The pulsing in my core is on the verge of unraveling as I lean forward, sinking my teeth into the neck of the man that instantly starts his release with the bite. That pleasure of the control and blood drives my body over the edge to my orgasm.

Darek is at the point of needing satisfaction as he watches. I puncture my wrist with my thumb ring, letting Darek drink of my blood in a small amount to taste and feel my orgasm. Darek instantly orgasms with the taste and feel from my blood.

Only I would have this ability as the original vampire. Now I need to figure out where all of these vampires are coming from.

Darek made sure that I knew how to find them if I need anything. Darek now has a mental connection with me, sharing my blood with him. If the donors were to have their blood mingle with mine, then they too would become vampires. Mortals cannot drink blood. The body cannot break down the blood cells in digestion, therefore making them sick. I laughed at all of the fairytales that said, if a vampire bites you, you become a vampire. So not accurate. Where did they get their information anyway?

Chapter 16

Sterling: Investigation

I had been doing my own investigating while Azalea was out feeding. The moment her teeth entered the flesh of the woman, I was at attention. I sat in the chair incapacitated from the erotic images I was receiving. Her orgasm brought me to my knees with needing her body now.

My need so powerful, I lean back in my chair to undo my pants. I wrap my hand around my already hard cock. I slide my hand up and down in rhythm with the feelings I am receiving from her. I can imagine that it is Azalea riding me, biting me. The thoughts of the erotic feelings of her bite flood over my senses causing me to orgasm with a force I have never felt.

As the images and erotic feelings of Azalea feeding start to subside, my thoughts return to the matter at hand.

I didn't know what was in the safe behind the large desk in the basement. I had never been permitted to enter the safe, even as an adult. I wanted to know what had to be kept, such a secret and why was it such a secret?

Dirk, Betsy, and Tim had still not returned. I knew nothing of their safety or if they are in trouble, until I hear the sweet voice of Betsy and that of Tim calling out my name.

I rise from the over-sized leather chair to head for the staircase. By the time I get to the base of the staircase, Betsy and Tim are descending the stairs. Both have a look of guilt and frustration on their faces.

"Sterling, we are sorry to have scared you like we did. We need to sit down and talk with you. It is time." Betsy and Tim led them back up the staircase to the kitchen. I sit at the table as Betsy starts the water on the stove for tea. Tim returns moments later with an ice pack.

"Where is Dirk? Have you seen him? What has happened to him? He was with me in the basement earlier when the attack happened."

"There is no simple way to tell you this Sterling. Your grandfather was supposed to be the one having this conversation with you. Not me." Betsy grabs the three teacups from the cabinet, filling them. With her own blend of tea, she has always made it for us.

"I am starting to feel like you are going to have the birds and bees conversation with me. I think I may be a little too old for that." I attempt to laugh, causing a splitting headache to take over my laughter. The moan that escapes my mouth doesn't help to decrease the pain either.

"I really need to go lay down for a while. I cannot concentrate on what you are going to tell me, that is so important. Come check on me in a few hours please if Azalea isn't back. She has gone out to feed. She will hopefully be back soon so she can hear what you have to say too. I'm sure it has to do with her in the end game. I just seem to know some things."

I crawl carefully into my king-sized bed, lay my head down carefully as I let the darkness consume my confusion and pain.

The back of the man's head came into view more as he blinked to get his eyes to focus again. The pain cut through his brain each time he opened his eyes. The slice of the dull blade cuts through once more as he keeps his eyes open at a slit, the pain reduced somewhat.

The dark hair slicked back as he wore a crown. Funny how you notice the small things. The crown, gold but plain, was somehow crooked on his head. Maybe it was the way he stood with his head slightly tilted. He leaned against the chair as he stood there with his back to him.

He tried to move his hands, unsuccessfully though. His hands were handcuffed to an eye hook in the tile floor. "Where is she?" The man turned around quickly to the sound of Sterling's voice.

"Well, you are alive. I was starting to wonder if you might die Sterling. That is a nasty bump you have. If you would just mind your business like a good boy, well, you wouldn't be here in this mess."

"You really don't get it yet, do you? You are a smart man, Sterling. Think about it. You will get it if you just think about it for a minute. What were the stories that your grandfather always told you? There once was a little boy…. Anything yet?"

Sterling's mind wandered back to the days he lay in bed while his grandfather told him stories before he went to sleep.

"There once was a little boy that would need to save the world. That little boy had a gift that he could see into the future, just like a wizard. The little boy would start seeing his future after he meets his eternal love."

"That little boy would meet the person who started all of the adventures his grandfather told him about. The one that his grandfather was so interested in all of those years, obsessing over. Your grandfather made sure to help you find her. We knew that he would do it. I had looked for her for hundreds of years unsuccessfully."

"It was foretold of a descendant of Elzabus having the ability for foresight. It is obviously not your father or grandfather were the ones blessed with this gift of foresight. The reason why I have had to wait patiently forever, it seems, is the vision of you being the one that would find Azalea. You are her eternal love."

"I have watched and waited through your entire lifetime. I watched you grow up to only be there for you daily. I watched as you discovered your gift and didn't even realize it most of the time. You have never truly understood the abilities you have or even the want to use them."

"Azalea is not the only one that Arawn struck a deal with. It was over a thousand years ago and I still remember it like it was yesterday." He paced around the small dimly lit room with the door having a window that told of many bright lights. The floor of tile was cold and unforgiving to the back.

He stalked to a small table with a chair, pulling out the chair to sit with a huff.

135

"My grief for such an action brought Arawn to answer me. In my grief, I swore to find the one responsible for my grief. I knew exactly who I was looking for though. Arawn laughed as he spoke of letting the games begin." He ran his hand up to go through his hair. He obviously forgot his crown on top of his head. He grabbed the crown roughly off of his head. Holding it in front of himself, looking at it. His hair messed up from dragging the crown across his head.

"This crown was made for my son that Azalea took away from me. She killed him the night he was to take over as the king. I planned on retiring to a good life of food, wine, and women." He slams the crown down on the table. "She took all of that away from me. The bitch will pay for what she did. I have no love left within me. I don't remember any love. I just know that when I get what I need from her, I will torture her slowly."

He got up to walk across the room to the door. He stopped as his fingers wrapped around the door handle. He didn't look back or move besides talking to Sterling. "You will die along with her." Turning the knob, opening the door, leaving with the slamming of the metal door behind himself. His head threatened to explode with the impact of the slam.

I shot up to a sitting position in the bed, dripping sweat from my brow. My pillow wet, and a form of my body remained. The remnants of the dream or vision possibly linger in my mind.

I get out of bed to go to the shower, only to be startled by Azalea sitting in the chair by the bed. "Holy shit you scared me. What are you doing?"

"Watching something interesting. Your visions could definitely use some fine tuning. The details are what we need, not your focus on Dirk being the jerk, King Carazus. He attacked you and you nearly didn't make it. We need to find him, not talk to him. I have been waiting for literally over a thousand years to kill this man. The sun is rising now, I need to get some rest so we can go find Carazus, or Dirk as you call him."

"We don't know for sure where he is."

"I have a way and place to find out. When I awaken, we will go find out."

Chapter 17

Men of the Past

I climb into the bed that Sterling had left. The sight of the man getting out of bed made me want for him again. His defined chest and stomach made him a beautiful specimen of a man. I decide I rather like the shaved and well cared for look. Not to mention that he always smells so good. A dark patch of hair covers his chest with a trail leading to the inside of his pant line.

The visions of Sterling's hard body helps to make my mind rest for the battle ahead. I had fed and now need rest. I decide that I will need to eat again when we go to find the information about Carazus that we need, like where he is.

The need is once again all-consuming to my soul to seek my revenge on Carazus. The darkness of vengeance rears its ugly head once again. The dreams and visions of my past come in waves of tears, followed by the rage of a thousand men. The presence of Arawn in my mind causes me to open my eyes to the darkness of the room once again.

Arawn lurks just beyond every corner, waiting for me to come to him, to provide the souls for him. He has his own minions for that now. He has not kept his part of the agreement; I don't owe him anything.

Sterling had been exploring the vault in the basement. The artifacts have all been from when Elzabus had been the wizard for the king. The relics are amazing for their age. His grandfather had traced and tracked down everything that he could on Elzabus. His grandfather was obsessed; one could say.

Sterling is so enthralled by what he is looking at, that he doesn't hear the approaching entity behind him. As a cold chill washes over Sterling, the realization that he is not alone hits him hard. Like a hammer to the head. A tall dark human-like figure appears before Sterling. Before he can speak, the figure has him against the wall by his throat. No sounds escape his mouth as the figure squeezes his neck to the point that he is gasping to breathe.

Sterling feels himself slipping in and out of consciousness. A pressure to his chest takes the rest of the oxygen from his lungs. The pressure so great the blackness takes what is left of the light in his eyes.

Arawn did not take his soul. He entered into Sterling. Arawn has always wanted to taste the sweetness of a human body before. The opportunity never presented like it does today. Not to mention that he gets to have his prized possession and object of his desires, if only for a short time. His experience with Azalea would be pure bliss without the threat of death. The chance to possess a mortal comes with the cost of the possibility of death. Mortality becomes real for Arawn or any other immortal.

Arawn opens his eyes to see the vanishing of his own body for now. He will need to call upon his body again when it is time to return to it.

The strength courses through his veins, as he moves the parts of his new body. He watches as his hands open and close with tan, not translucent skin covering the bones and flesh. The strength within that grasp brings about a rush of adrenaline.

The rush of adrenaline causes him to get an erection from the excitement. He knows all that

Sterling knows now. He knows exactly where to find Azalea and what to do with her for their satisfaction.

He reaches into his pants to rub the length of his newfound source of pleasure, hard and aching for Azalea. The more he thought of her, the harder he became. Only one thing could sate his pleasure now.

The end of the bed sinks down as he kneels on it after slowly pulling the blankets back. She wore no clothes in bed. Her body so glorious and the source of his desires at the time. He had been able to appreciate the beauty of her body one other time, when she took the prince's, rather, new kings life. He had watched her take her pleasure from his body before she sank her teeth into the neck of the pathetic human.

His hand reaches out to touch the top of her foot. His other hand follows suit on the other side of her body. He closes his eyes to feel everything. The end of the bed gives in to his weight as his knee settles between her feet.

Her skin so soft to the human hands he uses to feel her as he has desired to do. The ecstasy takes over his mind as the human body quivers around him. The shivers of erotic feelings soothes this mind. The sound of a moan escapes her lips causing the shiver to take over again. So sensual and heavenly is the thought that crosses his mind.

His hands travel over the tops of her knees to circle into her inner thighs. The sounds of satisfaction from Azalea continue to invade his senses. The realization that this is more satisfying than the souls he consumes takes over his body as he strips his clothes off quickly.

The pain in him is the sweetest pain he has ever felt. His lips touch her stomach to let his tongue touch her sweet skin.

The actions he takes are that of the memories of Sterling. The man knew what he was doing to draw out the sounds and reactions of her body. The mortal body is as magnificent thing. The memories of even the muscles in reflexes.

The need to move his mouth lower takes over his actions. The need to touch and taste every part of Azalea floods over his senses. As his tongue comes out to touch the hot, wet core, the feeling of satisfaction runs through his body in waves as he knows that he would never last long enough to pleasure her or himself fully.

As his tongue enters her core repeatedly and circles her hardened clit, she plunges her hands into his hair to grab two handfuls. The pleasure of her actions is too much as he wraps his hand around himself to move it up and down the shaft, having his orgasm hit him as she whispers his name.

Her hands pull him up and over her body for her to crush her lips to his to taste herself on him. The fire within him continues to rage a fire in his lower stomach. His body hard and ready once again. Wrapping an arm around her thigh he lifts it to push the tip in, then the rest slowly, savoring every nerve ending firing. Her hot wet core welcomes him with the pleasure they seek.

The actions of in and out weren't as pleasing as the circling of his hips to rub around her hardened clit. The heat of their bodies connected fuels the burning. She lifts her hips to meet the movements, increasing her pleasure. His hand moves down to put pressure on her hardened clit, circling slowly, causing her to moan louder and louder until her body orgasms with a force of its own.

The pure pleasure washes over both of them as she sinks her teeth into his neck, while riding out the last of her orgasm. The instant pain and pleasure hit within him so hard that he is forced from the body of Sterling.

"Well, I have to say. It's a good thing you let Sterling do the driving for that one. He is an incredible lover so far. Now you see what you are missing. If I had thought that Sterling was anything more than a meal, you would be dead, my Lord Arawn. Now you will tell me where Carazus is at so I can do what I have wanted to do for so many years. You kept him from me and now look what you have created. A monster much worse than myself.

"Carazus called upon me after the death of his son, Vincent. He of course offered himself to me for vengeance of the death of his son. I knew it was you and I waited for him to take your life so I could have you by my side for all of time as my queen. You have been the queen of blood and souls for so many years." His form returning to what it has been. He holds his hand out for Azalea to take it.

"I really hope you don't think I am going anywhere with you. I want what was promised to me so long ago." The anger seethes inside of her with the arrogance of Arawn. She gets up from the bed, getting her clothes on. She turns her face from him in disgust. Arawn disappears within his cloud of black smoke.

Pain seers through the scalp of Azalea, as she had never felt. She is held up, as a rope is twisted around her body from neck to ankles. The blackness of the cloth over her face calms the pain somewhat.

Chapter 18

Azalea: Where is Sterling?

The aroma of the blood makes me need for blood, seeping into my soul. The smell of the blood is that of Sterling and my own. I call out to Sterling. "Sterling are you there? Answer me." I knew he was not there. I hoped I was wrong, but right at the same time. I attempt to mind-link with Sterling, but there is nothing. He is obviously still out from when Arawn had taken over his body.

I connect to Darek. I need help to get myself untied and to start the search for Sterling. The connection is becoming weaker with each hour. I need him here now. The sound of the glass breaking upstairs and the wisp of the air next to me said that the reinforcements were there.

I count five bodies to be present with Darek. The more the better. I need to find Sterling before it is too late, hopefully it isn't too late already though. There isn't enough blood to make me think that he has been killed in the house, but enough to make him weaker, especially after he had been possessed by Arawn. He is probably the consistency of a wet noodle right now.

As the ropes that bound me fall away Darek and the others bow to me. "Our queen. What can we do for you?"

"We need to find out who was here and took Sterling. There is a familiar smell among the ones that took Sterling. I do need to feed though. I need more strength to fight more vampires and Arawn."

The other vampires with Darek audibly gasp as I say the name Arawn. "Don't be tricked by the name or the fact that, yes, he is a God." I run my hands through my thick blonde hair to pull it back into a ponytail. "Take me to the theatre to feed." I pull my hood up over my head as they all exit the front door to move with the speed of the light and sounds. I am not quite strong enough to transfer myself yet.

The door opens as they approach it. They had known the queen was returning to feed. Whispers of the Gods present have the club in an uproar as the entourage comes through the doors with the queen in the lead.

I walk up to the closest couch to lift my leg, heeled boot into the chest of a human donor. "You stay there, I will get to you next. While my leather clad leg and high heeled boot on the chest of the muscle-bound man, I motion with a long, elegant finger for a woman with large perfect breasts, a small waist, and dark auburn curly hair.

The woman approaches with a smile that makes my lower stomach, ache for the woman to touch me. As she stands in front of me, I place my finger under the woman's chin to lightly run it down the pulse that pounds in her jugular. The smell of the sexual tension in the air palpable between myself and the woman.

My gaze goes from the eyes of the woman to her lips that she licks sensually, to biting her bottom lip, moaning softly, causing the stir in me to burst into a million pieces of desire. My lips crush to the woman's with a hot passionate kiss, taking her breath away.

I break the connection between us, to turn the woman to sit on the man's lap, facing me. I move my hand sensually down the length of the woman's jawline, along her pounding artery carrying her life's blood, so rich and warm.

The woman reaches up to untie the strap around her neck to drop her shirt, exposing her perfect breasts. Her head tilts to the side as she reaches around to pull her hair out of the way. The man's hands come up to rub her nipples. Azalea kisses the woman deeply one more time before the woman purposely cuts her lip on Azalea's tooth, with a moan so sensual it sends all of my senses into overdrive. I sink my teeth into the neck of the woman to drink greedily, as the woman moans beneath me. The euphoria of the rich crimson blood and the orgasmic release makes me throw my head back to scream.

Not quite sated with my hunger yet, I lean around the woman to sink my teeth into the neck of the man we are seated on. I wrap my long fingers into his hair to hold his head as he moves more. Sated by their life's blood, I get up from the lap of the woman. My senses return to me as I think of the smell of Carazus' blood once again.

"Where have they taken Sterling? There is something going on here. Arawn has not made all of the vampires. None of you have made a deal with Arawn for immortality, have you?" I look around the room to all of the vampires. "Tell me what is going on."

"Carazus has a building that he has been using to do research and produce vampires from. We have all come from there. He only keeps certain people. Others are permitted to leave. We have found each

149

other. We can go to the building. It is actually an abandoned hospital on the outskirts of town." Darek bows before me once again. "You are our queen. We are here for you as you need us. You are the mother of the vampires."

The group of vampires transport themselves to a block away from the old hospital. "We are going in to see if we can get any information. Do not take any chances with the life of Sterling. He is to be unharmed at all costs. Do you understand me?" The group all nod in agreement.

The group approaches the building as quietly and quickly as possible to not be detected. She needs to know if Sterling is in there. If she can get close enough, she can mind link to him.

I creep along the wall of the building. The cool of the stones emanates through the robe to make my flesh prickle, every hair standing on end on my body. The sounds of the others around the area invades my ears as I concentrate on every sound. The distance holds the sound of screams at bay. The sounds of the city gone with the distance. The night air crisp and clean away from the city pollutants.

The light of the moon assists with the group of vampires headed for the door of the building. The doors are all locked up tight at the abandoned hospital as they would expect. The chain link fence surrounds the property, boards cover all of the windows where there had once been glass. The only thing that looks off is the bars on the windows to the lower level.

Jumping up and grabbing hold of the stone window frame, I notice that bars cover the other windows as well. The access points will be difficult to determine. This night is a scouting venture if needed.

The smell of the blood drives me to near madness. There was something different with this blood I can smell though. It is like an addiction I didn't even realize I have. The delectable smell of the blood drove the others to the brink of madness as well. I motion for the group to retreat so the mission would not fail before it started.

Chapter 19
Azalea: The Hideout

Azalea and the others return to the theatre to regroup all that had come along. The residual of the intoxicating smell leaves all of the vampires in a feeding frenzy. The sun on the horizon means that the hunt for Sterling will have to resume in the evening.

Before drifting off into the sleep of the undead, I cast a spell to be able to speak to the God's of History or Hecate, to search within my dreams for the answers to the questions I seek. Normally my sleep wouldn't consist of any dreams. This time I need answers though.

The sky purple as my eyes open fully. Laying on my back in a meadow. The clouds took the shapes of symbols I have seen before. A light breeze spins around my body, kicking up the pieces of the flowers and other debris in the vicinity. The sun is shining brightly above. The sun that has evaded me for so long. The warmth on my skin, not burning as it would have been any other time.

A crack of thunder breaks the silence and reverence that I enjoyed. Lighting reaches all around me as I watch the sun remain high in the sky as the black and gray billows of clouds form overhead. The sound of the continuous thunder deafening.

A form of immense proportion and glowing body, so brightly that I had to squint my eyes and raise my arm to shadow the light, approaching from in front of me. The form of a man comes into shape before my eyes. The man, enormous of size holding his spear and shield absorbed all of the lightning strikes.

I knew in that moment, my dreams and spell had called forth the God Lugh, the Shining One. God Lugh the sorcerer, healer, and warrior. His long blonde hair and beard moved in the breeze.

His presence seemed to set my soul on fire. The burning in my veins near intolerable. The healing elements of God Lugh alone made my body burn. My curse of the undead called upon Lugh for healing. I stepped back several steps, kneeling on one knee to the God before me.

"My God Lugh, I ask for the help for the souls of all of humanity. I don't think humans deserve this gift, but I will do what I need to save my love, Sterling. I ask for the strength, knowledge, and ability to save him. I call upon you as my God and sorcerer."

The voice boomed as he spoke. "I cannot heal your soul. You abandoned it to God Arawn. He has not fulfilled his end of the contract. You will know what to do when the time comes. You are the Queen of the Underworld. You will be blessed with the knowledge of the ones that wish to destroy all of mankind."

With those words spoken, God Lugh turns around becoming the blinding light that had approached me. The billowing angry gray and black clouds dissipate into the oblivion, leaving me confused in its wake with the sun once again upon my face.

My eyes open to the darkness of the theatre. The deception of the time, as it remained dark constantly in there. The sun would be setting in about another hour.

I try to mind link to Sterling once more. This time Sterling answers when I call to him.

"Where are you, Azalea? Don't come here. I don't know where I am for sure, but please don't come. You are in danger from Dirk. Well, I found out he is Carazus."

"I thought I smelled his blood. Are you sure it's not a descendant of his?"

"He told me that he is Carazus, he made up the name of Dirk. I know all about the stories of what he had done to your village and the rest of the landowners in the area. It is by his fault that you are the vampire you are today. I didn't say anything to him about you. I do miss you though. We haven't been apart much since I found you. There are a couple of people wanting to keep us apart."

"I will find you Sterling. I won't let anything happen to you this time." Feelings of possessiveness that I had never felt before came over me in a flood of feelings. *This time, I just said … this time.* The magnitude hit me. I had once lost the love of my life to the tyrant. Not ever again.

Chapter 20

Sterling: Sterling in Trouble

His eyes a slit as they open to the brightness of the lights. The tearing pain threatens to split my skull in half. The world makes no sense to me. What exactly is going on? One minute I am reading something, then I see myself making love to Azalea. Now I am tied up inside of some kind of a hospital type room. The area looks as if it had been an operating room. The equipment that litters the room looks ancient and unused for many years.

The buzz of the fluorescent lights is enough to drive a man mad, let alone the flickering. The pain in my head holds me on the edge of sanity as I wish for the pain to stop. Somehow, some way it needs to end. I decide to focus on something other than the pain of my head. My hands are tied behind his back with a zip tie nearly cutting off the circulation.

I nearly cry out for help. Like in the movies, either no one ever hears you or the wrong person comes to quiet you down. Neither option a good one. Sit here and focus on getting the pain to subside is the number one thing to do. I will have time to sort it out after I can make a rational thought.

I inhale deeply to count slowly to three. By the time I reach the count of three, my struggle with the churning of my stomach was lost. The nasty bile and other contents splatter to the floor to my right. I moved my head just in time to not wear my stomach contents.

Spilling my guts didn't help to make the pain any less. The movement actually increased the pain by tenfold. The scream escapes my lips, as I hope and pray for death to take me.

The scream did get the attention of someone. Not the good kind as I imagined. Dirk walks through the door to tilt his head to the side, looking at me.

"The first possession is always the worst. Drink this and you will feel better." Dirk holds the edge of the cup to my lips, tipping back the contents quickly. "Swallow quick, it tastes bad."

At this point in time, I don't care if I am drinking piss, as long as it makes the pain in my skull stop, even calm to a tolerable headache.

"Thank you, Dirk. My head is already feeling better. What is that? You could market that and make a fortune."

"I have amassed quite the fortune in the last thousand plus years my dear boy. Money is consequential to the power of being the king once again. This time it will be over the entire world, not just an area."

"Dirk, what the hell are you talking about?"

"You still don't get it, do you? Let me tell you a little story my dear boy. You may understand a little bit better." He walks over to the other side of the room, swishing the plastic curtain aside to grab another chair from against the wall.

"This version is going to include the details, but I really don't have enough time to explain the last fifteen hundred years to you." He sits the chair in front of me, so that we are face to face leaning on the back of the chair.

"Once upon a time. No just kidding. I won't do that to you." His chuckle echoes down the halls of the medical facility.

"There was once a witch that disappeared before I could kill her. I would have had her head on a platter with her body strewn across the land after it had been burned.---I really liked her that much.---I would gladly drink her blood from her boiled skull."

With a sadistic grin, he whirls the chair around to be sitting in the chair, his chest to the back of the chair.

"Why don't you untie me, Dirk? These damn zip ties hurt my wrists and ankles. "

"Oh, about that. I don't think I will be doing that. I will leave the ties on. I have no idea to what extent you will go, on any of this. By the way, my name is Carazus. I used that silly name for your benefit. Anyway … Let me continue my story."

"I once had a son. He was so much like me. He was following in his old man's footsteps, per say. He was going to be a great king, but the worst thing possible happened to us, we met Azalea." He ran his hands through his hair as he rose from the chair and started to pace back and forth.

"The night of his twenty first birthday he was crowned as the new king. Just after the ceremony he was killed by the Dearg Due or vampire to you, Azalea." He stops pacing, looking intently at me.

"She took my son from me; she is going to pay for what she has done. She will come for you; I know she will. When she comes for you, I will be waiting. I have plans for her. There is reason for her death, you will see."

"Don't you hurt her, or I swear to the gods, it will be the last thing you do! You have been lying to me this entire time about who you were? You were just

159

using me to get to Azalea? All of the stories I have read about the type of king you were, were real. You are a damn tyrant. You deserve everything you get. Fuck around and find out, Carazus, you will pay."

"Ah ha, I knew there was a reason I kept your hands and ankles tied. Women are just trouble all around. Either they cause you a problem or they are one. I guess I may have learned a thing or two in my long, long life, my boy."

Chapter 21

Azalea: Preparing for the Rescue

The sun slowly descended behind the buildings that tower on the horizon. The cast of the pink indicates a perfect night to rescue Sterling. The moon high in the sky, full and pulling the power of the vampires and witches alike.

The issue remained of the smell that nearly drove everyone to the brink of insanity to feed. Is that how he was luring the vampires to remain with him?

The local coven of strong witches and warlocks had come to the theatre while the vampires slept. The coven had been working hard at preparing spells to help in the mission to rescue Sterling.

The Grand High Priestess, Anissa bowed down onto a knee, followed by Elzabus at her side when I enter the room.

Within the blink of an eye, I am in front of Elzobus. My hand wraps around his throat as his feet dangle just above the floor. He gasps for oxygen but doesn't fight the darkness that is closing in around him. A hand touches my shoulder to bring me back to reality.

Elzabus drops to the floor as I turn away, taking a few steps back. I can't even look at him without wanting to kill him. He is someone that saved me but brought hate in me with the same breath. "I need to know why I shouldn't take your pathetic life from you now? Immortal until now, you would still die."

"Azalea, I did what I must to keep you alive. No matter how strong you were and are now, Carazus would have killed you." Elzabus stays on the floor kneeling before me.

"How is it possible that you are here now? How is Carazus here now too? The world has been turned upside down." The frustration evident on my face. I turn to face him once again. "Tell me everything. We need to rescue Sterling in a short time."

"I can help with that. I am the one who he has been using for more than a thousand years. He is probably just now figuring out that I am gone. If I had known he had someone of importance to you, I would have attempted to free them. I know what Carazus is capable of."

We enter the club area to sit and talk until it is time to leave. The plan has been discussed. I feel as if my nerve endings are set ablaze to understand what is happening.

"I have attempted to keep as much as I can as a secret from Carazus. He has kept me alive all of these years to make him more powerful." Elzobus paces back and forth in front of the table until I scream, "stop pacing," to him. He sits in a chair by the table I am sitting at immediately.

"The day on the mountain was the day that everything changed. I had landed on the ground below your tomb as I was attempting to prevent Carazus from owning my soul." He ran his hands through his gray beard. "My immortality came later than Carazus.' You really aren't going to like any of what I have to tell you, but I have to tell you none the less."

"I knew that you were going to take the life of his son Vincent. I foresaw what was going to happen. I of course did not tell Carazus or Vincent of my vision. You my dear were going to be the savior to our people."

He takes a deep breath as he hangs his head. "I found out from him, that when you had taken Vincent's life, Carazus had summoned upon God Arawn to seek vengeance upon you for Vincent's death. A servant to the king had seen what happened to Vincent from the doors."

"The day I was to die, I had died. Carazus had summoned upon Arawn to revive me to help him to become stronger and more powerful. My memory was taken from me for some time after the fall. The blessing in disguise for your sake."

He stood once again without pacing. "Carazus made a deal with Arawn to kill you. He gave Carazus more strength than you had, more enhanced powers than you, because Arawn wants you dead so he can have you beside him in the depths of the Underworld as his queen. The only way to have you is for you to voluntarily go with him or to die."

I saw red as the crimson took over my vision with fire running the length of my veins. The deepest recesses of blackness filled with the fire of my anger.

I rose so quickly that the table that once sat in front of me spun completely to land on it's top. Two other men approach quickly to grab me. Before I had time to think about anything, I had drawn my blades to slice so deeply that I had nearly beheaded the two men. Standing over the men with the anger controlling my mind, I run the swords through their hearts to finish the job.

Every person, whether they be vampire or human moved slowly to the walls. "There are obviously traitors among us. The evils of Carazus will be reconciled by the edge of my blades."

"Is there anything else I might need to know?" I place the tip of my blade under the chin of Elzabus, forcing him to look upward at me.

"The agreement was that Carazus would once again be king, not just any king. He would flood the world with vampires to become the king of the world. I heard one of the research scientists state that your blood is special to what they are doing. Your blood holds the cure. He who holds the cure, controls the world. They want your blood too."

"Well, I will give them all of my blood on the floor to have the chance to kill Carazus."

The final ray of sunlight narrowed until gone. The indication that the time had come to rescue Sterling. "Does everyone have their nose blocking ointment? I want to make sure that everyone knows. No matter what happens to me in there, Sterling will make it out of there alive." The coven spent all day preparing an ointment that would mask the smell of whatever they had in the lab.

165

They are all aware of the fact that Carazus and everyone would know they were on their way to the lab tonight. The hope remained that I had killed the only two traitors at the club already. Some element of surprise would be the best.

Darek and the others indicated they were ready for their directions from me. Within the blink of an eye, we stood a block away from the abandoned hospital.

Elzabus stayed behind with the coven. He gave the group directions around the hospital and where everything was kept. The pentagram on the floor was surrounded by the witches of the coven to attempt and keep everyone safe on the rescue mission.

Chapter 22

Azalea: Trouble

The feel of the cold hard bricks upon my back felt familiar. The same route had been taken as last time in an attempt to rescue Sterling. Darek was the first to enter the building through the side door that Elzabus had told them stays unlocked. He indicated that the area was clear as we all entered the building.

Elzabus informed us that if someone is being held in the building, they are always taken downstairs to the old surgical unit.

The group moves quickly through the halls of the building. I feel a sudden pull, almost like a call out for me to a room along the way. The small window in the door allows for me to look into the room. People lay on cots hooked up to tubing. They appear to be sleeping, or dead. The smell of fresh blood invades my sense of smell, even with the spell. The smell not as intoxicating as it had been though.

Darek mind links with me to find out where I am. I had been separated from the group. Just as I am turning to leave, the pain of the cracking of my skull causes the room and hallway to fade away. No thought has the ability to permeate the pain. The world tips on its side as the floor is hard and cold.

The screeching and sounds so familiar. Could that be a Dearg Due? How is that possible? The rushes of cool wind pass over just as quickly as the sounds surround her body. The spirits of the Dearg Due hostile and unrelenting in their anger. Azalea watches through slitted eyes as the world turns black and cold as ice.

"We need to go back and find Queen Azalea. She is not answering me." Darek directs some of the group to continue while he takes a few men with him to find her.

Images float through my mind in shear seconds. The flashes of the past invade my thoughts. The smells, sounds, all so familiar. It's feels like it is yesterday, so cliché.

Within my darkness the reality that the sluagh is there and imprisoning me. Carazus must have made them his slaves after all of these years. It seems that Carazus is getting stronger by the minute. The sluagh, the other vampires, and now whatever he is doing. The Gods only know what he is doing.

The familiar sounds and smells drag me down the rabbit hole of my past. So many years and lifetimes have passed since the ability to truly dream had passed.

Dreams of the past invade my mind.

I start to undress as Vincent watches. His eyes darken with lust as he matches my movements of taking clothing off. In a few moments we are both undressed as the servant had helped me to unlace my corset in a timely manner. I walk my naked body toward the steaming water.

The strong arm of Vincent comes around my waist, holding tightly. I look over his shoulder as I see many of the girls are staggering around the room with the servants attempting to assist them. I cast another spell, "all that occupy this room are to follow suit of the wine."
Vincent roars in my ear, asking what I said. "Nothing my king. I was simply purring in your ear. I was hoping you

would choose me to return to your chambers with you." I purr the words into his ear as I breathe in deeply of the scent of his blood.

King Vincent has the body of a king, such a waist of great human flesh on such a vulgar man. His erection stands perfectly at attention as I lower myself onto him. He lays back against the side as I move just enough to cause him to moan. He attempts to lean up to grab me as I push him back, slapping his hands away. He growls with acceptance as I ride him until the tightening in the pit of my core is ready to unravel.

Vincent reaches up, grabbing a handful of my hair with one hand as he wraps an arm around my waist. His mouth descends onto my neck as the unraveling starts. The servants and other women are all passed out around the room. My eyes turn crimson as my teeth start their descent. My teeth sharp and my actions quick.

My core starts to unravel at my climax as I sink my elongated teeth into the neck of Vincent. His immediate reaction is to wrap both arms around me and squeeze. I bite harder as he continues to lose more blood with his heart rate increasing. My orgasm reaches a new height with the combination.

Vincent stops fighting so much as he is weakened from the loss of the blood, I have taken in from him. I pull my head back to feel the pulse of his body inside of me as he orgasmed as well. "Such a waste. We could do this more often. I cannot let you go yet though. I need to make you suffer as I ride out what you have left within you. You remain hard from the rapid loss of blood, except from the area holding blood. Too bad your heart and brain are not the same way." I move on him again as the water sloshes around us. His eyes roll back as he attempts to talk. No words come out, only a moan.

I continue to build to my orgasm again as I plunge my teeth into the other side of his neck. I drink slowly as I feel my release again. I look into the cloudy eyes of King Vincent. "You will never hurt another again. May you not rest in peace. The soul eater has come for you. Your black, hideous soul is no longer your own."

The dream trailed off to the feeling of floating, like on a cloud. The sun was going up and down like every tick and tock of the clock.

Chapter 23

Sterling: Rescuing Sterling

I open my eyes to the sound of footsteps on the floor in front of my slumped over body. I had lost consciousness while my arms are bound behind the chair, ankles to the legs. I can no longer feel either my arms or legs.

The tinking and buzz of the lights had finally stopped though, until I opened my eyes again. My mind hung on the brink of madness and the abyss of despair.

Several men untied me while a couple other men kept a look out. I try to stand by himself, without success. My arms and legs dead.

"Slow down turbo. You aren't going to be walking by yourself anytime soon." The man says to me with a chuckle. "Let us help you. We are going to be moving fast. Keep your eyes closed." I was held up by a man on either side of me.

"Hurry, they are coming." The men try to move faster as they are dragging Sterling along. I keep moving my legs in an attempt to walk. "Stop trying to walk, you are only slowing us down." The urgency echoed through the words. Reality struck like a sledgehammer again.

The man to the right of me was hit from the side as the attack began. Unable to stand on my own, the man to my left and I went sailing into the wall, hard.

The tiles on the wall cracked and shattered to fall to the floor with an awful sound as the next wave of the attackers hit hard.

By this time Darek had heard the commotion. He came around the corner to stop a vampire from slashing my throat. Several men lay bleeding on the floor that soon turned to a pile of ash from their death.

I remembered a spell in the book about strength. I closed my eyes in an attempt to remember the words written down. Thank the gods for the ability to have a photographic memory.

I envision the page to see the words of strength. "To thine own body be true, let thine strength be one hundred-fold."

I felt the magic take over my body as I was able to jump up and assist with the fight for the lives of the ones that saved mine.

I ducked out of the way of a fist that came out of nowhere. The fist made contact with the tiles, making them shatter. The next fist came forward to hit the wall as well. During this swing I was able to make contact with a fist to the stomach of the man. He sails backward to return at me. I swing around to wrap my arm around his neck, successfully breaking the bones.

All that remains of the vampires were Darek and one other man. They grab hold of me and move with the speed of light out of the side door they entered.

Elzabus and the rest of the coven met me and Darek at the doors of the theatre. The wounds that Darek and the other man had obtained were nearly healed.

The coven members have Darek put me within the circle of salt made into a pentagram on the floor. The candles lit at each point of the star with a coven member present.

I was at the point of passing out again when I fought it off. Elzabus held his hand over my forehead as he spoke words that did not make sense to me at first. The spell gave me the strength to remain conscious.

The pain in my body started to dissipate with the humming and odd whispering of the coven members. I have never really studied the occult or other religions very much to understand what was going on with the coven.

With each moment my strength returned. There were several moments of intense pain as the muscles and tendons heal.

"Where is Azalea? Why isn't she here? Where is she?" I panicked at the thought of Azalea vanishing again. I could feel her though. Somehow, some way I could feel her.

Elzabus steps forward, sitting near the pentagram. "Tonight, with your rescue she has somehow been taken by Carazus. He has been waiting a very long time to get his hands on her."

"How could you guys let her be taken. Who left her there? Why was she allowed to be alone or in that situation? I would have died there in order to save her life." I turn to Darek. "Did you let your queen meet her demise. That is exactly what is going to happen to her. She will be treated like a lab rat until they kill her. After she is dead, they will call upon Arawn to take her soul and humankind will perish, due to your stupidity.

"She was the one who set up your rescue. During the entrance into the building, Azalea had gotten separated from the group somehow. Several went back to locate her when you were attacked. They had not located Azalea. She made it clear that no matter what, you were to get out of there alive."

Chapter 24

Azalea: Azalea's Capture

Pain courses through every nerve ending of my body. I try to focus on anything other than the pain. I listen to see if I am alone while squeezing my eyes shut from the pain. Being ran through with a sword wasn't even this painful.

I assess everything about my surroundings. I don't hear anything around me, other than heartbeats, many of them. I see the light through my closed eyelids. I am laying on a cold hard surface.

I can feel the tension and scream building in my body with the pain. My eyes fly open to the bright white lights. UV lights in a small amount surround my entire body. I struggle with my bonds to free myself from the torture.

The room filled with the stench and smoke of the scorching of my skin. The outer layers of skin burnt through to produce holes and blisters in my skin. Why must the UV light have such an effect on my skin?

The voice from behind me makes me scream. I feel the breath by my right ear from the familiar voice.

"Well, hello my dear. You have no idea how long I have waited for this moment." The smell of his breath makes my stomach turn, over the smell of my burned flesh.

I turn my head away from the stench of Carazus. "I bet you have waited almost as long as I have. Make that over one thousand years you asshole." The slap to my face reverberates through my entire skull as my teeth clang together.

I struggle with the bonds to my wrists, ankles, and neck once more. The UV lights dim to nothing more than the light of the fluorescent bulbs overhead.

I can move my head just enough to see that I am wearing a hospital gown and all of the other metal slabs, holding others down, tubes in and out of their bodies.

Several other people approach that have lab coats on. I suppose they are the scientists that will do the research on me and my blood. I struggle against the silver that burns my skin with each movement. The rubbing of the silver causing more anguish. Unable to move, I lie still to glare at the scientists, memorizing their faces so I can track them down later.

"I hope he has paid you all very well, because I am going to kill each and every one of you."

Another slap comes to my cheek. "You would be wise to shut that pretty little mouth of yours, before I shut it for you." Carazus chuckles sadistically. "It would give me great pleasure. Get her ready for the move. We need to get going soon, before any more of the idiots come looking for her."

With Carazus walking away, I am stuck with the first needle to withdraw my blood. The scientists don't speak nor look me in the face as they continue to examine me more. I am injected with something that immediately makes me sleepy, overtaking me. That's when I hear the other voice that I recognize as Vincent's. *That's impossible,* is the last thing I think before the darkness takes me.

I somewhat wake up. I have no idea if this is just a dream, or if it is real. I am strapped to a chair, a wheelchair specifically. I can feel the straps across my chest. The silver handcuffs remain on my wrists, attached to the frame of the chair. My eyes only slightly open to see. My ankles bound to the foot pedals. My head hangs and stretches my neck muscles to the point of pain.

I attempt to lift my head to see where we are. The area is dark around me. I can't see anything for the fog in my vision. I blink a few more times to clear my vision. No success as someone states that I am awake. I feel the poke of the needle into my arm.

I realize before the dark consumes my mind that I am in a vehicle. I can hear the slight rumble of the exhaust and the road is bumpy. My struggle against the darkness taking over is a losing battle as I drift back off into the darkness.

My eyes flutter open to the sounds to my right. Another round of scientists with white coats to take more blood, prod me even more. *They keep me on the brink of death as they make sure to keep me asleep. If they want me dead, what is holding them back? They can only take so much blood from me.*

I attempt to focus my thoughts to mind link with Darek or Sterling. The drugs they have me on are not letting the fog lift long enough to get a thought out.

"She has opened her eyes. We need more of the sedative. We are needing a larger dose. She seems to be building a resistance to it. It's lasting for shorter durations now."

Well, at least my body is fighting harder than my mind. Eventually the sedative will not have any effect on me. Hopefully that time comes soon. Everyone knows where I was, but no way to get to me now. I woke up once to being moved. I was taken to a different location. That would mean that no one will know where to find me.

A feeling of defeat and doom settles into me. I have lived for over one thousand years but only just started to live again. The darkness lonely now without Sterling next to me. I can't get my mind off of him now. I will let the memories of my time with him carry me through. The moment of clarity let me envision Sterling in his handsome form.

If you can hear me Sterling, I was moved somewhere else. I don't have anything else I can tell you. The darkness is approaching once again. They are keeping me at the point of death and sleeping.

The thought was gone within moments of having it. The drugs were taking effect once again. I realized I didn't know how long I have been out of it. *How long have I been here?*

My eyes flutter shut once again to have the darkness, now my best friend, take me into its arms once again.

Chapter 25

Sterling: Vault Room

I sit at the desk looking over the piles of papers and information that grandfather had accumulated over the time of his research. I want to bang my head on the desk to clear the thoughts of what could be happening to Azalea as I sit here.

A knock comes to the doors of the library. Our main area of operation was moved to the estate after the rescue. My body is sore and battered from my time with Carazus, but I am home, without Azalea though.

I shout in anger with my thoughts fueling me, "come in."

The door opens slowly to Elzabus treading softly on my nerves. He is dressed in a suit which does nothing for the imagination that he is a great wizard that holds great magic.

"I think it is time to see what your grandfather had hidden in that basement for all of these years. We may find something that will help us."

The trek down to the basement has my mind reeling at the fact there was a place that grandfather had hidden from me all of this time. We found Azalea's swords in his collection he kept secret.

The wine cellar has a chill to it as I reach the landing. I stop just long enough to recognize the feeling that my grandfather had given to me when he was too close to me. The touch of a spirit causes that electrical charge for the skin to prickle and raise hairs.

I whip my head around to look at Elzabus. "Did you feel that? We aren't alone. There is a spirit in here."

"I did feel it. Let me go first. I will perform a binding spell for the spirit. After it is bound, we can vanquish it."

Elzabus holds his hand out while he casts a spell. I am familiar with the spell that I had read in the book of his. I start to chant the words along with him before I know what I am doing.

Before we descend the stairs Elzabus turns to look at me with questions written on his face. The look of confusion made me realize what I was doing.

The cool air seems to stop moving. The air thick, making it difficult to take a deep breath. A crushing feeling surrounds me as we reach the bottom of the stairs. The white gray mist from the apparition lingers in the air of the office.

The closer we get to the apparition, the more I can make out the features of it. The apparition has dark hair, tall, and broad. It reminds me of Carazus. *Maybe Carazus is now dead, and he was able to find his way back to the house after all of the years of being with us.*

I approach quicker now out of curiosity. It is not Carazus as I got closer, but it definitely resembled him. I startle at the sound of a sigh behind me. I am lost in thoughts about who the spirit is.

"Sterling, I want to introduce you to Vincent. The son of Carazus."

"This is impossible. How can a spirit last for that long without moving on?" My hairs on my neck and arms stand with the electricity. The spirit watches every move I make, unable to move from the spot he is in. He stands just inside of the vault area behind the desk.

Elzabus looks around the room to all of the artifacts in glass prisons. He went to touch the first case nearest him. The electricity of the zap he receives can be heard and seen.

"Your grandfather put a spell on the case holding anything he thought to be of value."

"I have no idea what my grandfather has down here. I was not even aware that this place existed until

185

recently. Grandfather kept it a secret from me. I can touch the cases is all I know from when I was down here with Azalea."

"This is something that could be of great value to us Sterling." Elzabus points to the case without getting close enough to touch it.

I stand beside Elzabus looking into the case that holds a large gold medallion with a purple stone in the middle. Writing surrounds the stone of ancient Celtic. I can't read the writing due to it has been a lost language.

Elzabus starts reading the writing surrounding the stone. "Third eye of God Balor, may he be the seer of all that remains evil." His look of surprise let me know that this is something of great value. "Where did your grandfather find something like this? Holy shit."

"I have no idea where he was able to get anything in this room."

"This is something that was lost to the Gods. This is the medallion that can summon and control the God Balor. He is a malevolent leader to other malevolent spirits. He is the oldest of the Gods. He has been depicted as a cyclops in history and fairytales. He has the one magical eye. The third eye. He is the seer over all of evil." Elzabus shifts uncomfortably next to me.

"It has been said that once evil returns to the world that God Balor will return to reign over all evil. Carazus is thinking that once he becomes king again that God Arawn will protect him from Balor. I did not tell him otherwise. There are some battles that we pick. That is one that I choose not to participate in. I would like nothing more than to see the demise of Carazus."

The case next to the medallion held a gold dagger with jewels encased on the handle. Elzabus stops next to me to have a sharp intake of his breath. "Your grandfather was definitely a man of many means. This dagger is the dagger of life. This dagger belongs to the Sun God, Lugh. He is considered to be the Shining One. He was always the sorcerer, healer, and warrior. He was a great God. The God Balor that I spoke of, well, this is his grandson." I step back with all of the information received by Elzabus.

"You must see all of the similarities of you and your grandfather. You being a relation first off, he was in the sluagh, a malevolent spirit; then you have Lugh which is the sorcerer and healer, just like you. There is too much coincidence." I walk away so I can breathe better. The air was not thick like it had been before. I was just in shock from all of the information that Elzobus was giving me.

I wander around the room looking quickly at everything until I come to a large case on the floor in a circle of salt. "Elzabus, what is this?"

"This is a case to trap a spirit. The salt will prevent it from leaving the case. I don't see any spirit in there right now. I guess we have somewhere to put Vincent."

An incantation from within the book came to my memory. I look to Elzabus that knew what to do as well. I ran upstairs to return after a few minutes. I carried a bag of rock salt from the garage for the cold days that produced ice or frost.

I start to make the pentagram around the outside of the circle with the rock salt. We both held hands around the container while chanting the binding spell. "Spirit contained to stay in this case. Let the salt hold you here." We both watch as the spirit of Vincent enters the case. The chills come over me with the apparition passing by me. I can tell this spirit is evil and strong, just one of us would not have been able to control him.

"You are definitely the wizard of the family now. I bet you are a stronger wizard than I am now. I'm sure Azalea is as well. I can do a few tricks, but you are a natural in all ways."

Chapter 26

Azalea

The once cold hard slab was better than the accommodations at this time. The wheelchair I am strapped to left me slumped over and in pain.

Just as that thought went through my mind I am being moved again, after my head is shoved back once again. The smell of more blood sends my senses into a frenzy. I have not fed in god knows how long. The hunger racks my body with pain, but the weakness is the worst part of it. The loss of blood and hunger is almost too much for me to handle. The weakness holds me back from doing what I must.

A slap comes to my face. I am shocked by the action I wasn't expecting. I open my eyes slowly to look up at Carazus.

"Where is it that Sterling could keep him?" The anger evident as he spit while he talked. His face went from a slight blush to a purple in a matter of seconds with the amount of rage emitting from his body.

I continue to watch his face filled with rage as he slaps me across the face again. No sound escapes me as I feel the blood trickle down my chin. The weakness has taken all energy from my body.

At this rate I will bleed out the rest of my blood before he get an answer from me. I attempt to raise my head unsuccessfully. All I can do is sit there with my head hanging, with my blood dripping from my bottom lip.

"Sir, she is too weak to answer you." A shaky voice comes from behind me. I hear the fear within their words. I recognize the voice as one that I have heard many times, a soft female voice.

"Get her strong enough that she can answer my questions. Vincent has been captured; I know it. I need her to give me information. Work fast. Your lives depend on it."

People scramble around me. I hear the shuffling of feet as the darkness lingers all around me. I am going to die. I feel what life I have left in me leaving. I was once immortal and thought invincible. I guess I have been proven wrong, once again.

The feel of being picked up and being laid on a table brings my thoughts back from my inevitable grave, momentarily. My body strapped down once again to the cold metal slab of a table.

The end is in sight as the tunnel forms before my eyes. I relax my body to let myself go. My last thoughts are not of myself, but of Sterling. I envision his chiseled features, with memory of his square jaw, a day's growth for that rugged look. The straight nose leading to the most mesmerizing hazel yellow eyes.

The dark waves of hair hanging over his eyes partially. I want to reach up and move his hair back. The full lips that I have savored open slightly as if to tell me something. I focus on the movement of his lips. My mind is not functioning like it should be.

The smell of blood invades me like a vivid memory of the past. The feel of the warmth spreads across my lip and into my mouth. Several more drips follow the first. My tongue darts out to my bottom lip as my teeth elongate with my hunger for the sweet, warm, sticky blood.

I open my eyes to see a thin arm above my mouth; cut to have the blood dripping out. I stretch my neck to go toward the source of the sweet blood. The wrist comes down just enough for my mouth to connect to the source. My teeth penetrate the soft skin as the warm blood fills my mouth; I drink greedily.

I hear the soft voice that had echoed behind me earlier. *That is enough. I can't give you anymore.* She pulls her arm away as I open my mouth further. *Since when did I become soft? When did I start caring what anyone else wanted? I have never succumbed to the whimpers of my victims. It is amazing what a near death experience can do to your judgement.* Confusion plagues my mind as I lay back again.

Saved from the clutches of death, this girl offered her blood to save me from my death. I need to see her face. I would be willing to spare her life when I am free of my confines. Her face heart-shaped with pretty brown eyes. Her brown hair pulled back into a ponytail. Her glasses slid down her nose for her to push them back up.

Carazus storms into the room, pushing the doors open so hard they bounce back toward him. A quick hand comes out to catch the door before it hit him. The people all around the table jump with a start at the sound of the slamming door. He stops just inside of the doorway to look at the metal table holding me. A sneer crosses his face as his sights are set on me.

"Where would Sterling have Vincent? How would he have captured Vincent? I take it that is where Elzabus has gone too. He better hope that he is doing some recon for me. I will kill him too. The only reason he is alive is because of me. I saved his ass from death. Maybe not his wretched soul though." He circles the table where I lay. Looking at my face the entire time.

"I have no idea what you are talking about Carazus. I haven't even seen Vincent."

"Don't try to avoid the question."

"I'm not avoiding it. I have no idea." My mind wondered as I thought about it. I really had no idea where Sterling would keep a spirit.

Carazus had asked me another question that I didn't answer due to my mind wandering. I feel the sting of yet another slap to the face. I open my eyes again to look at him. The look of contempt on my face must have screamed as he took a step back.

Chapter 27

Sterling

Elzabus and Sterling stood in the vault in awe of the objects they had found from grandfather. "I probably don't want to know how he obtained most of the artifacts that he has in here."

"Vincent is now securely locked away. We don't need to worry about him now. I can't imagine what the hell Carazus had to do to keep his sons spirit in the world with him.

I look over to Elzabus with a guilty look on his face. "I know how he did it. I'm not proud that I helped all along with him remaining on this earth for all this time." Elzabus walks out of the vault with me in tow of him. He plops down into one of the large leather chairs of the office.

"Carazus was able to keep the spirit of Vincent around when he made his deal with Arawn." He ran his hand over his long gray beard.

"When I stepped off the side of that mountain so that Carazus' men would not catch me, he had God Arawn present with him. He had made a deal with Arawn to make himself immortal to find and kill Azalea. He called upon him with the discovery of his son Vincent. He had been dead long enough that he was no longer within his body."

Elzabus stands and starts to pace back and forth in front of the desk. "Arawn is not able to bring someone back after they have been dead for so long. If the spirit has left the body, all he can do is summon the spirit and keep him bound. You see, Vincent is bound to his father. This is the only way that Vincent has been able to stay upon the earth for so long."

Elzabus stops in front of Sterling, leaning back onto the desk. "You aren't going to like this part. Carazus has been counting on his son being of flesh and bone once more. He just needs the perfect host."

'Then why hasn't he brought Vincent back in a host yet?"

"It's a little bit complicated." Elzabus huffs as he once again starts to pace.

"The host has be a reincarnated spirit of whom Azalea loves and would give her life for."

"What the hell are you saying? I am supposed to be the host?"

Elzobus stops midway in his pace, not looking at Sterling. "That is correct. You are the reincarnation of Thomas, and Azalea loves you. The timing is now perfect. He needs to have you and the blood of Azalea to have you become the perfect host for Vincent. Once Vincent has taken over your spirit, then he plans to kill Azalea. He won't kill her until he has used her to create the serum for the cure of vampirism though." He resumes his pacing, this time around the room.

"He has been making vampires though. Why would he want a cure for it? That doesn't make sense at all." I shake my head in disbelief.

"I know one thing for sure. He better not kill her, or I swear by the Gods, I will rip him apart."

"He is looking for that reaction from both you and Azalea for this to work. He is planning on using Vincent within your body to kill Azalea."

"We need to get to Azalea now. We need to get her out of that place. Get everyone together once more."

Sterling knocks on the door to the club and theatre. The door opens for him as he walks down the hall to find Darek. He needs to get the help of all of the vampires to save Azalea.

Darek stands at the bar talking with other men gathered around him. No others were in the club besides them.

"We need to get to Azalea, now."

"I was wondering how long it would take you to decide to save our queen, Azalea. We were just making plans on what we were going to do to make our attack. I'm sure by now they are locking that door that we came through before." Darek held his hand out to shake mine.

I am in amazement that they were going to go rescue Azalea when this is probably a one-way mission for all of them; me included.

We move over to a table near us that had a map on it. It is the schematics for the hospital when it was built. "Where did you guys find that?" I asked with confusion.

"We have our ways." Darek exaggerates a smile at me.

"So, what are you thinking?"

"We are looking at the front door honestly. Attack from the front. We need to use bolt cutters for the chain. There is nothing blocking the doors. I noticed that when we were there before. It would be perfect for a fast and undetected entrance. We need to

197

time it just right so that the camera is turned out of the direction of the front doors to make our entrance. We will have to have a few people at a time to prevent detection."

"The plan sounds good so far, but we will need to have a way to shut this place down too. That lab needs to be done with its ways." I run my hand through my hair in frustration at the thought of the lab continuing to make more vampires and torturing people to do so.

"I need to warn you though Sterling. The new vampires are in a feeding frenzy, and they are a hundred times stronger than even we are. If one of them get ahold of you, you may not live. I need you to stay behind me. Don't try to be a hero."

"We will meet you back here then after the sun goes down. We will be ready to go."

Chapter 28

Sterling

The sun is on the horizon as we decide to leave the estate and go back to the club to meet with Darek and the others. We have approximately twenty men in total for our rescue mission. I have so many questions for Elzabus. I don't know where to start. I decide after we rescue Azalea, I will sit with Elzabus and ask hm all of the questions that flood my mind.

The drive back to the city is somewhat quiet. The anticipation of the rescue makes me fidgety.

"Sterling. There is something I do need to tell you. Darek was the first vampire that was created by Carazus. He obtained the blood from God Arawn to help him in the creation, for yet another soul in payment. I just want you to know how old and strong Darek is. He should be able to protect you when your magic cannot."

The remainder of the drive I sat there quietly. I decide that I could totally trust Darek now.

All of the men stand in waiting for us as they are ready to fight a war for their queen. I often wonder why Darek had called Azalea the queen, how he knew about her. I now have my answers to some questions.

The old hospital comes into sight. We have parked down the street to keep from being detected. Just as Darek had said, there are cameras that would rotate for a view of the entire front of the run-down building.

The first person is up at the door cutting the chain as the rest of us watch and wait. He has the chain cut and entering the building in a mere moment. We aren't going to have a problem getting in. It is going to be Elzabus, and I that may take too long.

I am the last one to get in, besides Darek that insists that I stay behind him. The men fall into single file as they walk along the walls slowly and quietly. Not a single man made a sound as we descend the stairs to the basement, surgical unit. The door is opened quickly and quietly. The scientist in their white lab coats sit at tables. No other vampires or Carazus in site. The nearest scientist screams as she turns around, seeing all of us.

The other scientists and lab coats turn to watch us move upon them. I struggle to the front of the group with Darek on my heels.

"Where are you guys keeping Azalea? Where is she?" I grab the girl by the throat, squeezing just enough that she starts grabbing at my forearms. I release her just enough that she takes a deep breath.

The girl looks toward Elzabus then back to me. She repeats her action again as Elzabus nods yes to her.

"They all left, they took the woman with them. We are the only ones here." I yell to the men in the back to check out the rest of the hospital and keep us informed. The hospital is big enough that Darek decides to have all but me, Elzabus, and one man stay behind.

I let go of the girl to have her rub her throat and take more deep breaths.

Darek and the others leave the room as I sit down in the nearest chair, looking at all of the people that lay on the metal tables with tubes in and out of their bodies. They make me think they are dead, except for the heart monitors showing their heartbeats.

Elzabus paces the area as he did at the estate. He continues to mumble something that I can't hear. I lean

forward with my elbows on my thighs to rub my face.
The cracking sound reverberates throughout the room
as I hit the floor in a pile.

Chapter 29

Sterling & Azalea

Sterling's eyes open just enough to see. The floor is coming at my face faster than I can respond, to break the fall. The concrete floor is cold and unforgiving. I spit a mouthful of blood out from biting my tongue with the fall.

Noises to my left indicate I am not alone on the concrete floor. Darek lay a little ways away. He looks more uncomfortable than I did, as he is handcuffed with silver cuffs, causing burns to his wrists. His feet bound with silver as well. We are both laying there not moving or talking as Elzabus clears his throat.

"I suppose I should thank you my boy. You are the key to things."

"I'm going to kill you when I get my hands on you." I struggle against my ties.

"Not before I have a chance at him," comes out in anguished words from Darek.

"I thought I could trust you Elzabus." I spit toward him again.

"Sorry my boy, but I have a soul on the line with all of this. I am in a fight for my soul too. I just find mine more valuable that I do yours. Now that you have spoken your peace, you don't need to speak anymore. No spells or anything from you." The duct tape is slapped across my face by Elzabus before I have a chance to say anything more.

Elzabus walks out of the room, giving orders to some men to get us ready to be moved, with a smug look on his face. I instantly roll towards Darek. I move my jaw around just enough while rubbing the tape on my shoulder to get it down just enough to move my lips.

"I have seen when vampires change, they have their teeth and fingernails elongate. Am I correct?"

"You are right. Why do you ask?"

"I need you to break out the fingernails. I will lay behind you and I can cut my ties on my hands. When I am free, I will free you."

"I'm not sure I can do that with the silver handcuffs. The pain in my wrists is too much right now."

"I need you to concentrate and work through it somehow. Azalea needs us right now."

The plan didn't have time to work as we were both grabbed, lifted up, and drug to a vehicle. We are both thrown into the back of a large vehicle.

I eventually get myself turned as much as I can to get our hands in the same area. I push my hands against Darek's, so he knows that I am ready for him to try to get his fingernails to elongate for me.

The tip of a fingernail runs across the palm of my hand as I move my hand up. The smell of the blood must have reached Darek as his fingernails instantly elongate to full length. I hear a small growl emit from his throat.

The vehicle is pulling into a garage, coming to a stop as the blood takes over what is left for strength of Darek's. The doors open just as he snaps his handcuffs, and my ties are cut.

I feel the warmth of my blood on my hand as I follow the lead of Darek that gets out and is automatically fighting with every person that comes running at us.

I am grabbed from behind as my reactions are also automatic. I swing around, causing the man to stumble away from me as I come around behind him, wrapping my arm around his neck. I lock my arms in place as I feel the sting of the knife enter my stomach. I hold as long as I can with the pain tearing through every nerve ending in my body, screaming in anguish.

The sting of the blade a couple more times is like a shock wave with each thrust of the knife.

I fall to the ground to see the red of my blood coming through my shirt. I press over the spots with both hands. I scream in pain as I push on them.

Darek has killed the other two men as he rushes to assist me, from hearing my screams. He rips the throat out of the man standing over me with my blood dripping from his blade.

The blood hot and sticky as it pushes out around my fingers.

Azalea lay on the cold metal table in nothing more than a thin hospital type gown. The effects of the blood I had received were wearing off now. I need to feed more than I did. The weakness keeping me going in and out of consciousness.

The blood draws and the tests continue at this new place I am. How long has I been here now? I have lost track of the days I have been held here.

Just as I start to close my eyes again, I hear the screams of Sterling. My eyes open wide so I can listen. Am I hearing the screams through a connection or is he close? The confusion is set into the source of the screams. All I know is that Sterling is in trouble.

The stabbing pain causes me to cringe with the pain in my stomach. The smell of his blood fills my nose as I breathe in deeply of the scent.

The realization comes to me that Sterling has been hurt and I am sensing his death. I close my eyes to focus once again. Sterling must be close for me to feel him this strongly.

The thought of Sterling dying brings out something in me that I didn't think possible. The love I had once felt was crushed with the death of my Thomas so, so, long ago. My heart now aches for Sterling. I have grown to love the man who saved me from my eternal sleep.

My mind takes over long enough to have my teeth elongate and my fingernails to protrude. The weakness in my body subsided some. Not enough to escape my handcuffs though. The silver draining all the energy I have left in my body.

I feel the tears roll down my face. I know there is nothing I can do to help him. The feelings of helplessness overcome me. All I can do is scream his name. I scream so loud that his name echoes throughout the room and my head. I can feel his life leaving his body. The words, "Azalea, I love you," going through his mind.

Chapter 30

Sterling & Azalea

Sterling hears the scream of Azalea for him. The scream seems to be close yet so far away as his blood continues to gush from around his hand. The walls of his vision start to close in as Darek leans over him.

"Darek, I need you to save Azalea. She is here. I feel and hear her. She must live. It is better this way. At least Vincent cannot have me."

"It can be different for you. You don't have to die. The woman you love is never going to age. She is going to have to watch you get old and or die otherwise."

"How exactly are we supposed to do this? You mean for me to become a vampire too?" I take in a deep breath to keep myself awake. I am starting to fade by the second. I can hear my heartbeat in my ears as the thump becomes more faint with each beat.

"Are you saying you want to be a vampire? Do you want me to change you, Sterling? I need a definitive answer from you. Say it now. I am willing to give you immortal life to save our queen."

"Do it now. I want to live and be with Azalea forever." The words starting to trail off.

Darek grabs a blade from the floor. He runs the blade across the palm of his hand, for the blood to run down the crease in his palm. The blood drips as he moves my hands off of my stomach.

"My blood mixed with yours is what you need to become a vampire. Not going to lie … this is going to hurt like a son of a bitch. Brace yourself for the change."

The floor of the garage shakes, as if a herd of elephants were approaching. The garage door that had been closed comes off of the rails in a single unit. The sound deafening as the effects of the change start for Sterling.

I lay there holding my stomach as it slowly stops bleeding. The skin starts to heal itself from the wounds. The pain in my stomach makes me grip at it once again. This time, cramping and a searing hot pain.

The sky turns black as night as clouds billow around a form, which is human-like, but much larger than average. The form wears a black hooded robe as it sticks out a large finger, pointing at me.

"You are not supposed to be here now. This is not part of the plan. That damn Carazus did this. You are supposed to be dead. You will not stand in the way of my queen and I." With a sound as loud as thunder he is gone.

My pain continues to rip into my sanity as I hang between life and death. My mind feels as if I am going to implode from the building pressure as my teeth elongate. The bones in my hands break with the sound of the cracking as they elongate for the first time.

I writhe in pain as Darek stands there watching what he knew to be painful. "Relax your body now Sterling. The worst is over. Let the pain leave your body as it must. We have to get to Azalea now."

A feeling or hunger you can say, comes over me like waves. I can feel the strength of a hundred men flow through my veins with a vengeance. My only thought is to save my love, Azalea.

The door into the mansion bursts open with about ten men flowing through. I can smell the metallic of their blood and hear their hearts pump their blood through their bodies. The thumping of their hearts drives me mad to feed as the smell takes over my senses. Darek attacks one of the men as I watch how to feed the right way. My strength caught me by surprise as the first man to me flew back against the garage wall when I struck him. I rush forward to fall in behind the man. I wrap my arm around his head as I tilt it, making his neck accessible.

I can feel his fear, smell his adrenaline and blood. I can see the pulse of his carotid artery in his neck pulsing to his rapid heart rate. A thrill buzzes through me of excitement as I feel my teeth enter the pliable flesh, blood filling my mouth faster than I can swallow it.

At first, I was almost sick to my stomach to get over the thought of the blood. My hunger for the blood insatiable at the moment though. All I can think about is getting more blood to drink.

Darek yells my name to get my attention. You need to focus on what we are here for now. It is going to be difficult to focus, but you must. Azalea needs us now.

As we enter the house, the basement door is readily accessible. Darek leads as we slowly descend the stairs to the basement. The smell of Azalea hits my senses light a hammer. I know she is here. We continue along cautiously.

I can feel, hear, and smell Azalea. The smell of the blood of others mixed in to make my mind crazed with hunger. I keep my mind focused on Azalea though. Her smell so delicious and enchanting.

I am so focused or crazed, I don't know which as we come to a door. Darek opens the door slowly for us to see the dark shadow once again, holding Carazus against the wall by his throat.

"You were not supposed to kill or injure the man, Sterling. Your idiots just killed him and now he is changed to a vampire. What can I do with that now?" Azalea lays on a table not far from them.

We enter the room quietly as Carazus lets out a bellow, alerting every one of us being there. The robed figure turns to us as Carazus drops to the floor.

"You will not have her. She is meant to be with me." The robed figure towered over us as the billows of clouds surround him.

I see Carazus and Elzabus trying to leave as I turn back once more. The wizard part of me kicks in. "You will not leave this room until I let you. You will stay." I slam the door shut with the motion of my arm swinging. Both men stop in their tracks to look like they are literally frozen.

The door reopens for several men to charge at us. I get to the side of Azalea just as a man tries to attack me. With one hand I pull her handcuffs off of her and the bonds on her ankles, while I hold the man there by the throat in the other hand.

Azalea sits up weakly, as she attacks and feeds off of the man, I am holding there in front of her. Several other men attempt to capture us as my strength is ten times of what they are capable. Azalea regains some of her strength as she rips the neck open of another man.

The dark figure remains there looking at Azalea.

"I have Carazus here for you Azalea. It's time you get to exact your revenge on the soul you have sought revenge on." He holds his hand out to Azalea. She blindly walks toward Carazus.

You can see the sweat beads on the forehead of Carazus as he knows his time has come for Azalea's revenge on him. Even though he sought revenge on her. His wicked sneer and death glare does nothing to deter Azalea from her mission.

"Azalea don't do it. If you kill him then your soul belongs to Arawn, and you will die." I try to talk to her, but she seems to not hear a word I have just said. "Azalea, you need to listen to me."

It is like the entire room is in a stale mate as the only one that moves is Azalea, who is slowly walking toward Carazus. The actions all appear to be in slow motion.

Azalea fights with her inner demons. The urge to kill Carazus fades more and more with the words that she hears behind herself. The voice of Sterling. He is now a vampire. He will be with her forever.

A clap of thunder shakes the room. Arawn loses his patience for his queen. "Kill him now my queen. He is yours for the taking. I promised you the death of Carazus."

The long arm of Arawn reaches out to grab Darek by the throat. The anger evident in Arawn's eyes as he watches Azalea. "You will complete our agreement and kill him now or I will kill Darek." Arawn boomed.

Darek struggled to breathe as Arawn held him above the ground, feet dangling.

"Times up Azalea." Arawn turns his full attention to Darek. Before she had time to move or say another word, Arawn moved quicky, shoving his hand into the chest of Darek.

Arawn pulled his hand from the chest of Arawn with his still beating heart in his hand. The blood flows from his body as Arawn tosses him with no regard.

Sterling had seen enough. Sterling uses his new speed and strength to move behind Carazus with ease, tilting his head and ripping the tissue of his neck so that his blood soaks the front of his clothing. Gurgling sounds make their way from the mouth of Carazus. "Now you can have his soul."

A terrible rumbling makes its way out of the throat of Arawn as he watches Sterling drop the body of Carazus to the floor. The billowing of the anger is deafening in the room as all cover their ears. The room dark and filled with black smoke.

"You will never have Azalea. She will never be your queen; she is my queen."

The billowing clouds, blackness and the smell of sulfur start to clear from the room. Azalea stands completely still, looking at the body of Carazus.

Sterling makes it over to the side of Azalea just in time for her to turn to him. A resonating slap stuns Sterling as Azalea turns to walk away. "How dare you take that away from me?"

Chapter 31

Sterling

It has been 4 days since the day Darek and Carazus died. Azalea walked out of the house and disappeared. I have been looking and waiting for her ever since, hoping she will come back to the estate. I can feel her inner turmoil.

Something flipped inside of Azalea that day. She realized she had feelings once again. She was no longer the puppet of anyone else. She is now free of her bonds with Arawn, and she has someone, me, to love her. I just need to give her the time to deal with everything.

If Arawn decides to return for Azalea, we now have a couple of medallions in our favor. Lord Balor or Lugh will be summoned if need be.

On the fourth day of looking for Azalea she came home to the estate. The sun had just set, and I was getting ready to leave, to look for her. I stand in place as I prepare for the worst from her. I took away her ability to obtain her vengeance. I made that decision to save the woman I loved. I knew her anger wouldn't stop her from killing Carazus.

I stand there as she circles me several times not saying a word to me. My eyes move but my body does not. At the next pass in front of me, I reach out, grabbing her. I crush her lips to mine as I hold the back of her head. I release the kiss as I move my lips to her neck, just below her ear.

I whisper to her, "I did what I did so I didn't lose you. I would go to the ends of the earth and back to be with you. You are my world. The rest of it can burn to the ground."

I feel her hands touch my sides as she snakes her arms around me. Her breathing heavy. I can feel her chest rise and fall with each breath.

I don't move as I cherish the feel of her arms around my body, hers pressed to mine. My lips find hers. I knew in that moment that my forever was secured with the woman I love.

The End

You can follow me on:

https://linktr.ee/ravenwatters

Facebook

Raven Watters | Facebook

Instagram

Raven Watters (@author.ravenwatters) • Instagram

Amazon

https://www.amazon.com/author/ravenwatters

TikTok

https://www.tiktok.com/@author.ravenwatters

Also Available on Barnes & Noble

9 7989 88 1 5 5 0 1 0